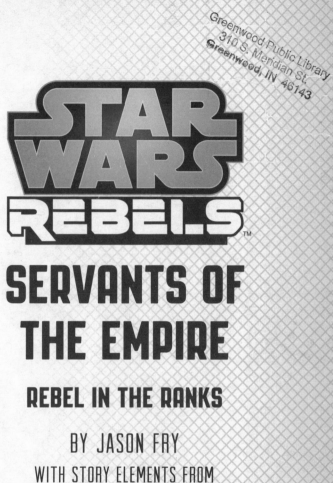

STAR WARS
REBELS™

SERVANTS OF THE EMPIRE

REBEL IN THE RANKS

BY JASON FRY

WITH STORY ELEMENTS FROM
THE *STAR WARS REBELS* EPISODE
"BREAKING RANKS," BY GREG WEISMAN

DISNEY

LUCASFILM

PRESS

Los Angeles • New York

Printed in the United States of America

First Edition, March 2015

1 3 5 7 9 10 8 6 4 2

Library of Congress Control Number: 2014954906

V475-2873-0-15016

ISBN 978-1-4847-1644-1

Visit the official *Star Wars* website: www.starwars.com

SUSTAINABLE
FORESTRY
INITIATIVE

Certified Chain of Custody
Promoting Sustainable Forestry

www.sfiprogram.org
SFI-01054

The SFI label applies to the text stock

To my own fellow cadets, who taught me how to (usually) catch a baseball and to eat ice cream first so you have room for it. You know who you are.
—J.F.

PROLOGUE:
THE INTAKE

Zare Leonis could tell the moment the Imperial officer read that Zare's sister had gone missing.

Sergeant Currahee was a squat, powerful-looking woman with a ruddy slab of a face and pale scars that snaked up from her collar and disappeared into her hair, which was the same industrial gray as her uniform. She was his intake officer at the Imperial Academy on Lothal, sitting across a bare metal table from him, a datapad in one meaty hand.

"The intake tests show superior reaction time and field of vision for a fifteen-year-old," Currahee said in her gravelly voice. "But you're consistently slow in selecting between targets, Leonis—you'll need to work on your initiative."

Currahee pursed her thin lips, her small black eyes scanning her datapad and then jumping to Zare's face. She put down the datapad.

"When you imagine yourself in Imperial service, what do you think about?" she asked, steepling her fingers and resting them against her chin.

For a moment Zare let himself imagine what would happen if he told the truth: That he knew the Empire had lied about his older sister Dhara's disappearance from this very academy. That Zare planned to pose as a model Imperial cadet while searching for Dhara and awaiting a chance to bring down the Empire. That he was in fact already an enemy of the Emperor's regime— he'd even thrown detonators at an Imperial troop transport.

He smiled to think of the shocked look that would transform Currahee's face, then realized her eyes were fixed on him.

"I just want to serve the Empire, ma'am," he said, forcing himself to sit up straight and adopt a bright, determined expression.

"And the issue of target selection, Leonis? How would you address that?"

"Uh, I guess I need to learn how to assess tactical alternatives better, ma'am," Zare said, running a hand through his wiry, close-cut black hair.

"So maybe the Imperial Army is right for you?"

"Whatever my superior officers think best, ma'am."

Currahee nodded without much interest, then picked up her datapad again.

"You were center striker on your school's grav-ball squad," she said.

"Yes, ma'am," Zare said. "We were league champs."

"You must have some leadership qualities, then."

Zare dropped his eyes modestly, then nodded. That was what a model cadet would do, he hoped.

"There are plenty of boys here with strong leadership abilities, though," Currahee said. "Suppose your superior officers determine you can best serve the Empire as a stormtrooper, Leonis. Would that be . . . *beneath* you?"

Zare thought back briefly to his neighbor Ames Bunkle, who'd entered the Academy with Dhara last year, then emerged as an expressionless Imperial drone, barely able to do more than recite parts of the stormtrooper manual.

"I just want to do my part, ma'am," he said stonily.

Currahee's eyes studied her datapad again, then jumped to Zare's face. Up and down they went between him and whatever was on her screen.

Zare knew at once that she had reached the part of his file that mentioned Dhara. He wondered if she was reading the same story Commandant Aresko had told

Zare and his parents last spring—that Dhara had run away during a training exercise. Or perhaps the truth Zare was seeking so desperately was on that datapad, less than a meter away.

He could rip the device out of her hands and read what it said—but it would be his last act before the Empire interrogated him and discovered everything.

"Your sister abandoned her Academy training," Currahee said simply, her eyes boring into Zare's face.

Zare managed not to scream that she was lying— that Dhara had been the loyal Imperial he was only pretending to be, and that she would never have run away without telling her family.

He ducked his head, forcing himself to master his emotions, then looked up to meet Currahee's penetrating gaze.

"Is there any news about her?" he asked. "My parents and I have been so worried."

He knew there wasn't any news—his girlfriend, Merei Spanjaf, had hacked into the insecure upper levels of the Academy's data network and would alert him immediately if his sister's status changed. But he still couldn't help feeling a flutter of hope. Merei couldn't see sensitive information. Perhaps Currahee knew something she didn't.

"The Empire is doing all it can to discover Cadet Leonis's whereabouts and reunite your family," Currahee said blandly, and Zare reminded himself that he couldn't give the officer any hint that he didn't believe her.

Currahee looked down at her datapad, then up at Zare again.

"Do you ever dream about your sister?"

"What?" asked Zare, startled.

"Ever dream you can see her somewhere, in a place you've never been? Or that she's calling out to you?"

Zare stared at Currahee, anger churning inside him. Then he shook his head slowly.

"Of course I dream about Dhara—she's my sister. But . . . they're just dreams. Why are you asking me this?"

"Just curious," Currahee said, tapping at her datapad.

Zare didn't know Sergeant Currahee, but he was pretty confident she'd never been curious.

"I'm recommending the standard orientation," she said, then extended her hand and offered Zare a thin smile, one that didn't reach her eyes. "Welcome to the Empire, Cadet Leonis."

PART 1:
ORIENTATION

Merei Spanjaf woke up when her datapad began warbling the familiar glissando that opened Plexo-33's oldie "With You Among the Stars." She hated that song so thoroughly that its first notes were enough to launch her out of bed and across the room to shut off the datapad.

Treacly ballad silenced, Merei pawed fitfully at her short, sleep-mussed black hair and settled into the chair at her desk, fumbling the datapad into its power cradle. She replaced Plexo-33 with the bass rumble of a heavy isotope remix and idly scanned the news from her hand-picked list of feeds. The Empire had obliterated a slavers' nest on Carrandar Secundus, Lothal grain production had exceeded ministry targets, and the Galactic League commissioner was reviewing a big proposed trade between the Shad Furies and the Eriadu Patriots.

How thrilling, Merei thought, yawning as she loaded

her messages. The administrator at Lothal's Vocational School for Institutional Security—V-SIS—had invited her and the school's other new students to an assembly about ethical practices in information security. She smiled as she added that to her calendar. If the administrator could see what she was going to do next, he'd be calling the authorities instead of summoning her to an ethics seminar.

Fully awake now, Merei tapped out a brief series of commands on her datapad, humming along with the thump of the music. The program she executed masked her device's ID, encrypted its transmissions, and rerouted them through several servers located elsewhere on Lothal. Satisfied that no one could trace her datapad's inquiries back to her family's apartment in Capital City, Merei began searching her usual list of Imperial databases for any mention of Dhara Leonis.

Merei didn't have access to any truly vital information, but the top levels of the Empire's various databases on Lothal were insecure, a product of the haste with which they'd been set up. Merei checked the Imperial Academy's records for Dhara and got the same answer she always did: Dhara Leonis's status was INACTIVE.

Curious, she typed in the name Zare Leonis, then smiled when the record came up ENROLLED.

Merei let her fingertip rest for a moment on her

boyfriend's name, wondering what he was doing. They'd parted two days before—Zare for the Academy and Merei for V-SIS—and Merei knew they wouldn't be able to talk for two weeks, until Zare had completed cadet orientation.

The song ended and Merei shook her head. Day-dreaming would make her late for school. She searched the Empire's law-enforcement alerts for any mention of Dhara, then the customs and identification-processing databases, then six or seven more she'd managed to gain access to over the summer.

There was nothing.

Merei sat back in disappointment, the heels of her palms pressed against her eyes.

"Merei, are you awake?" her mother, Jessa, yelled. "It's time to get moving."

"I know, Mom," Merei said, quickly exiting her concealment program and blanking her datapad's screen. She looked at the datapad in consternation for a long moment, seeing herself dimly reflected there.

This isn't working, she thought. *I can't reach the information I need. I have to go deeper.*

The thought frightened her. Her parents, Jessa and Gandr, were both data-security specialists who worked as contractors for a number of Imperial ministries. Merei had heard their tales of intrusions tracked back to would-be saboteurs and thieves. Most of them never knew they'd been caught until the stormtroopers arrived at their doors.

The prying she'd done into the Empire's networks was already risky. If she tried to penetrate the more-secure records, she was risking interrogation, detention, and worse.

Merei shook her head. It was dangerous, but Zare was in danger, too—he had willingly joined the Academy despite his sister having vanished during her service as a cadet. And their friend Beck Ollet was in Imperial custody for his ill-fated attempt at rebellion, his fate unknown.

She would have to try. She owed that to Zare . . . and to Beck and Dhara.

But not right now. Right now she needed to shower, and get a cup of caf, and go to school.

Before she pulled her shirt over her head Merei scowled at the inactive datapad, its screen a mocking blank.

Where are you, Dhara? People vanish into thin air, but information doesn't. There must be a trace some-where. I'll find it—and then I'll find you.

It was autumn on Lothal, but the summer heat still lay heavily over the Easthills, leaving the tall green grass shimmering ahead of the sweating, gasping cadets struggling up the slope.

"CADETS! MOVE IT!" barked Currahee, running back and forth along the line of cadets. The sergeant's gray shirt was dark with sweat and her face was red, but her short legs kept hammering along the paved roadway.

"Doesn't that witch ever get tired?" gasped Jai Kell.

"Apparently not," Zare muttered beside Jai. He turned to Nazhros Oleg and Pandak Symes. "Come on, guys, let's step it up before she hands out more demerits."

"Never mind Curry—what about Chiron?" gasped Jai, swiping at the sweat running into his eyes.

Zare followed Jai's eyes to Currahee's slim and handsome superior officer, Lieutenant Chiron. He was gliding gently along the roadway ahead of the cadets, not a hair out of place.

"He's not even breathing hard," Zare said in disbelief.

"That's because he doesn't breathe—he's *inhuman*," Jai replied.

There were four squads of cadets toiling up the hills. Each squad had eight cadets, divided into two units. Zare's squad was NRC-077, and he, Kell, Oleg, and Symes were Unit Aurek.

Chiron saw the cadets looking at him and gave them a cheerful wave.

"Beautiful morning, isn't it, gentlemen?" he said.

"But then every morning in the Emperor's service is beautiful! Every ration square's the finest nerf steak! Every bunk's a featherbed! Oh, to be an Imperial cadet out for a stroll on the beautiful planet Lothal!"

"That man's crazy—this is the worst morning on the worst planet in the whole galaxy," muttered Jai.

The cadets who could spare the breath muttered and groaned as Chiron ran effortlessly up the hill. Zare could hear Symes gasping behind him. He dropped back beside the slim boy, who looked glassy-eyed.

"Come on, Pandak—it can't be too much farther," Zare said. "Just focus on the next few steps."

"I don't think I can make it," Pandak managed through gritted teeth.

"You're right—you can't," hissed Oleg from the other side of the struggling boy. "You're a failure, Symes. Quit and go home."

The other cadet's predatory grin made Zare angry.

"Leave him alone, Nazhros," he warned him.

"I told you not to call me that," Oleg warned. "Pretty soon you'll call me 'sir.' For now, it's just Oleg."

Before Zare could reply, Currahee pushed between Zare and Pandak, glaring at the squad.

"Are you having a MORNING CHAT, Unit Aurek?" she bellowed. "Is the pace TOO SLOW for you, Unit Aurek?"

"No, ma'am!" Zare yelled, hastily joined by Jai.

"Apparently it is, or you'd be RUNNING instead of TALKING," she roared. "CADETS! UNIT AUREK WANTS US TO GO FASTER! PICK IT UP, CADETS! DOUBLE TIME! UP THE HILL!"

Zare groaned as the knot of boys began to run faster.

"Nice job, Aurek," gasped a pale cadet from Unit Cresh.

"Yeah, way to go, losers," another managed.

One cadet staggered off the roadway and clutched at his heaving stomach.

"Pandak!" Zare urged. "Stay with us! We're almost at the top of the hill! You can do this!"

Currahee had dropped back to scream at the sick cadet. He managed a shaky jog.

"WHO WANTS TO QUIT? WHO WANTS TO QUIT RIGHT NOW?" Currahee roared, staring at each cadet in red-faced fury as she passed him. "IT CAN ALL BE OVER IN A SECOND, GENTLEMEN! JUST SAY 'I QUIT' AND THE DROID TRUCK WILL TAKE YOU BACK DOWN THE HILL! BACK TO YOUR MOMMIES AND YOUR NANNY DROIDS! COME ON! WHICH OF YOU WORTHLESS CADETS WILL BE THE FIRST TO QUIT?"

Zare ignored the bellowing sergeant, but couldn't help thinking of his own mother, Tepha. He had told her what he'd learned—that the Empire was lying about Dhara having run away, and that they'd killed peaceful protestors and claimed they were rebels. She'd been aghast at his plan to follow Dhara into the Academy, only agreeing after he promised to desert at the first hint that he might suffer whatever fate had befallen his sister.

Then there was the Leonis family nanny droid, the ancient model known for generations as Auntie Nags. Zare wondered what she would think of Currahee.

That woman has no manners, he could imagine Auntie Nags sniffing, her photoreceptors switching from yellow to red. *Imagine, treating children that way!*

He allowed himself a grin—which immediately brought a furious Currahee to his side.

"WHAT ARE YOU SMILING AT, LEONIS?" Currahee roared.

"Nothing, ma'am!" Zare barked, eyes straight ahead.

Currahee settled in beside Zare as the cadets struggled up the long rise, her little black eyes fixed on his face.

"This is where your sister abandoned her comrades, isn't it, Leonis?" she barked.

Zare's head wheeled around to stare at the sergeant, teeth bared in fury.

"Leonis! I asked you a question!"

"Don't know, ma'am!"

"Aren't you going to do the same thing, Leonis?" Currahee demanded.

"No, ma'am!" Zare said.

"I don't believe you, Leonis! You're lying! Isn't that right, Leonis?"

Chiron had dropped back to parallel Currahee and Zare. He looked intrigued, but also concerned.

"No, ma'am!" Zare yelled.

"Yes, you are! You're just wasting the Empire's time! Aren't you, cadet?"

"NO, MA'AM!" Zare screamed.

On the way from the mess hall to the barracks that night, Zare dropped back from the crowd of tired cadets to walk next to Symes, who was trudging along by himself, eyes hollow with exhaustion.

"You okay, Pandak?" Zare asked in a low voice.

The other boy managed to nod. "It'll get better, right? It has to."

"It will," Zare said.

"You promise?" Pandak asked with a grim smile.

Zare clapped him on the shoulder.

"Yes, I do. Look, Pandak: my sister was a cadet last year. Orientation's when they try to weed you out. She said it felt like forever, but it's only two weeks. After that things get easier. We'll be in shape for the drills, and they'll lift the communications blackout."

"Are your parents worried about you?" Pandak asked.

Zare hesitated.

"My mother is," he said, thinking that for once he was telling the truth. Zare's father, Leo, still believed in the Empire as a force for good in the galaxy and had no idea what Zare had discovered about Dhara, or what he intended to do.

"What about your folks, Pandak?" he asked, hoping to draw out the anxious boy.

"They're not worried," Pandak said, shaking his head sadly. "My parents don't believe in failure. They're both career Imperial Army—Colonel and Major Symes. They told me this was my first stop—achieve honors here, then qualify for Arkanis Academy, or maybe Marleyvane. And then Raithal when I'm eighteen. Or Corulag at the very least."

Zare nodded. Lothal was a one-year junior academy, and its graduates would move on to a longer stint at one of the senior academies elsewhere in the Outer Rim. After seniors, the very best cadets would enter a specialized service academy for officer training with the Army, Navy, or Stormtrooper Corps, while the others would go straight into the Imperial military. Some would return to their homeworld to enforce the Emperor's will; others would serve him on any of the Empire's millions of other planets.

"Sounds like your folks have it all figured out for you," Zare said sympathetically.

"Yeah," Pandak said. "Except for where I wash out at the beginning of juniors and never even get off Lothal. That wasn't part of the plan."

Pandak was asleep even before lights-out, snoring softly in his bunk as Zare, Oleg, and Jai put away their toiletries and tagged their sweat-stained clothes for pickup by the maintenance droids.

Oleg, who bunked above Pandak, looked scornfully at his fellow cadet, then reached down and plucked something off Pandak's footlocker. It was a chance cube, Zare saw. Oleg turned it over and over in his fingers, teeth bared.

"There are red sides and blue sides," Jai said with a grin. "You roll it, and—"

"I know what a chance cube is," Oleg said, his voice rising. "I wanted that bunk, but Pandak won the roll for it. I bet he cheated."

"I don't think Symes is a cheater," Jai said.

Oleg dropped the chance cube on the footlocker and turned away, correcting a minute imperfection in his black hair.

"Maybe not, but he's definitely a loser," he said. "He should just quit. Before Currahee decides to have him for breakfast."

Zare started to say something, but decided not to—he was too tired to fight with Oleg, and sensed what the sour-faced cadet really wanted was to get a rise out of him or Jai. Better to starve him of the attention he craved.

"I don't think Curry eats breakfast," Jai said. "I think she lives on blaster gas and molten carbonite."

"Every meal a banquet," Zare said with a smile.

"Right," Jai said. "Finest ration-squares on Lothal. What I wouldn't give for a couple of maize rolls with genuine Westhills butter."

"You're from Lothal, then," Zare said.

"Born and raised," Jai said. "And ready to see the galaxy. You?"

"Here, there, and everywhere," Zare said. "I was born on Uquine, in the Colonies, but before we came to Lothal we lived on Hosk Station."

"A space station? Wizard," Jai said. "And what about you, Nazh . . . Oleg? Are you from here?"

"Of course not," Oleg spat, then became suddenly busy sorting his toiletries. "I'm from Eufornis."

"Which one?" Zare asked. "Eufornis Major, or Eufornis Minor?"

Oleg threw a look of hatred Zare's way.

"Minor," he said.

Zare nodded, unable to suppress a smile. Eufornis Major was a prestigious city-planet in the Core, but Eufornis Minor was an Outer Rim colony even more remote than Lothal.

"Why did your folks come to Lothal?" Jai asked.

"They didn't—they're dead," Oleg said.

"I'm sorry," Jai said. "My dad died a couple of years ago."

Oleg just shrugged.

"My uncles are freight haulers out of Eufornis," he said. "Import this, export that. They heard about the Empire's investments here and decided to pack up and move."

"Makes sense," Jai said. "A lot of new folks have come here in the last few years, looking for opportunities."

Oleg scowled. "Good for them—this is the only opportunity I need. Once I make one of the senior academies I'm never coming back to this miserable dirtball again."

Zare glanced at Jai to see if he'd take offense to this dismissal of his homeworld, but the other cadet just shrugged, then yawned.

"Well, the seniors will have to wait," he said,

lowering himself into the bunk below Jai's and prodding at the thin mattress. "Time for this cadet to hit his luxurious featherbed."

When the commotion began a jolt of adrenaline shot through Zare and propelled him out of the top bunk to a panicky stance on the floor, certain the people who'd made Dhara vanish had now come for him.

But it was Currahee, and she'd come for all of them.

"CADETS, ASSEMBLE! GET UP! I SAID GET UP, YOU PATHETIC PACK OF FLEA-BITTEN MONONGS!"

Zare managed to stand at wobbly attention, blinking at the glaring lights. Currahee's uniform was crisp and perfect, as if it weren't the middle of the night.

"SYKES! AT ATTENTION! WHAT IS WRONG WITH YOU, CADET?"

"Nothing, ma'am!"

"DO YOU WANT TO GO BACK TO BED, SYKES?"

"Yes, ma'am! Uh, I mean . . . no. No, ma'am!"

"I DON'T BELIEVE YOU, SYKES!"

"Symes," Pandak squeaked.

"WHAT?"

"It's Symes! Ma'am!"

"SYKES, SYMES—I WILL CALL YOU WHAT-EVER I WANT, YOU MISERABLE EXCUSE FOR A

CADET! DO YOU HAVE A PROBLEM WITH THAT?"

Currahee stared at the miserable Pandak, her eyes bulging. Beside Pandak, Oleg smirked.

"ARE YOU SMILING, CADET?" roared Currahee. "DO YOU FIND INSPECTION AMUSING, OLEG?"

"No, ma'am," Oleg said.

"FOOTLOCKERS OPEN, ALL OF YOU! NOW, CADETS! NOW, NOW, NOW!"

Zare and the others fumbled to get their footlockers open. Currahee marched back and forth in an increasing rage, hurling boots and gear and toiletries across the room.

"LOOK AT THE DIRT ON THESE BOOTS, KELL! LEONIS! IS THIS HOW YOU FOLD A FORMAL TUNIC? OLEG, THIS FLIMSI IS CONTRABAND! SYKES! YOUR TOOTH GEL IS UNCAPPED AND YOUR SHOWER SHOES ARE FILTHY! THREE DEMERITS EACH! YOU HAVE THIRTY MINUTES, CADETS! IF I FIND ANY INFRACTION—ANYTHING AT ALL—I'LL HAVE THE FOUR OF YOU RUNNING UP THE EASTHILLS BEFORE DAWN!"

Currahee found infractions, of course. The only comfort for Zare and his unit mates was that every other squad had suffered her wrath as well and also found themselves running in the predawn gloom as Currahee screamed at them and Chiron ran back and forth with his usual infuriating ease, as if getting up hours early to run uphill was a special treat.

Pandak was in trouble from the very beginning of the run, stumbling and then falling farther and farther behind the clumps of cadets.

"You can't help him," Jai said urgently when Zare glanced back for the third or fourth time.

"I have to try," Zare said, peeling away from the others. Currahee intercepted him after just a few meters.

"LEONIS! WHERE DO YOU THINK YOU'RE GOING, CADET?"

"Helping a member of my unit, ma'am!"

"IS THAT AN OBJECTIVE FOR THIS MISSION, LEONIS?"

Zare just stared at the furious woman. *Mission? We're running up a hill—the same hill we ran up yesterday.*

"HAVE YOU GONE DEAF, CADET? I ASKED YOU A QUESTION!"

"No, ma'am," Zare muttered.

"THEN GET BACK IN LINE!" Currahee screamed. "UNLESS YOU WANT EVERY SQUAD TO REPEAT THIS EXERCISE AGAIN! IS THAT WHAT YOU WANT, LEONIS?"

Zare was tempted for a moment, but saw the anger and desperation on the faces of the cadets around him.

After a last glance at the struggling Pandak, he reluctantly turned away from Currahee and ran back to Jai and Oleg.

Pandak was the last cadet to reach the top of the Easthills, running the final kilometer with Currahee at his heels demanding to know if he was ready to quit yet. The miserable cadet kept repeating "No, ma'am" weakly, and just shook his head when Zare caught his eye.

In the shower room before dinner, Zare set the water as hot as he could stand it and stood under the jets, hoping to work the aches out of his arms and legs. He racked his brain for something he could say that might help Pandak, then stopped himself.

Pandak's an Imperial cadet, he thought. *Why do I want to help him? To help him become an effective Imperial officer? That's not what I came here to do.*

He tried to ignore Pandak, but in the mess hall Oleg started in on the cadet immediately, his eyes flicking from Jai to Zare with each insult.

"Give me your fruit bar, Symes—you're not going to need it," he said. "Because you're going home. Because you can't cut it."

Pandak pushed Oleg's fork away, briefly angry. But Zare saw his eyes go glassy again almost immediately.

"Quit, Symes. You're not Imperial material and you

know it. Worse than that, you're an embarrassment to the rest of us."

"Shut up, Oleg," Zare said.

Oleg's black eyes jumped briefly to Zare.

"You gonna make me, Leonis? Didn't think so. Give me that fruit bar, Symes—"

Zare reached across the table and slapped Oleg's fork out of his hand. It skittered across the floor as the other cadets grew quiet. Zare saw Currahee's head jerk up from her tray where she sat eating with Chiron.

"Leave him alone, Oleg," Zare said. "Right now."

Oleg got to his feet and stomped around the table, ending up nose to nose with Zare. Currahee watched with interest but remained seated.

"I dropped my fork, Leonis," Oleg hissed. "You better go get it before I jam it down your throat."

Then Chiron was standing next to them.

"That's two demerits, Oleg," he said. "Sit down before you get a lot more."

"Yes, sir," Oleg drawled, his eyes not leaving Zare's.

Chiron watched him until he returned to his seat, then looked at Zare.

"My office, Leonis. Right now."

Zare followed Chiron down the hall, their bootheels ringing on the polished floor. Once inside his office, Chiron nodded for Zare to take one of the two chairs.

He removed his cap and set it down carefully, then settled himself behind the desk.

"You want to tell me what that was all about, cadet?" he asked quietly.

"Just a disagreement within my unit, sir," Zare said.

"It was about Symes, wasn't it?"

Zare said nothing. Chiron sighed.

"I may not agree with Sergeant Currahee's methods, Leonis, but she has a history of creating capable cadets," he said. "During orientation, a cadet may be humiliated by his or her failure. But that failure won't lead to death, or to the failure of a mission. In active service, that's no longer true. Do you understand what I'm saying?"

"Yes, sir. But Pandak wants to live up to his parents' example. And his dedication . . . well, it's obvious, sir. Shouldn't the Empire find a place for a cadet like that?"

"Perhaps," Chiron said. "No, not 'perhaps.' Yes, it should. But that's not the Empire the two of us serve."

They sat in silence for a moment. Then Chiron leaned forward, the corners of his mouth turned down.

"Leonis, I've read your file. You were accepted, declined your spot at the Academy, and then changed your mind. All this happened around the time your sister disappeared from the Academy."

Zare studied Chiron's face. The officer's concern

looked genuine. Before Zare could figure out what to say, Chiron spoke again.

"Currahee and I transferred here from Marleyvane over the summer, so I never met your sister," he said. "But I have trouble believing a star cadet like that would abandon the Academy with no warning."

"My parents and I had trouble believing it, too, sir," Zare said carefully. "But Commandant Aresko told us that's what happened. He saw to it that alerts about Dhara were placed in every ministry's database, in case she turns up. Now we just hope she'll make contact and say she's coming home."

Chiron nodded, his eyes on Zare's.

"It's a very strange case, Zare," Chiron said. "Let me make a few inquiries of my own when I'm at headquarters. Perhaps my role at the Academy will let me find something out that might be helpful."

Zare felt a flutter in his stomach. He didn't doubt that Chiron was sincere—but if the officer poked around within the Academy it might attract attention, imperiling his own efforts and putting Merei in greater danger.

But of course he couldn't tell Chiron any of this.

"Thank you, sir," he said, trying to keep the man from hearing the fear in his voice.

★ ★ ★

Oddly, Merei's big break came when her father caught her.

She'd been sitting with her datapad at the kitchen table after school and decided to check a couple of the databases she routinely visited in case some new information about Dhara had appeared. Almost of their own accord, her fingers tapped out the sequence that hid her inquiries' point of origin. She figured she'd start with local law enforcement, and typed in DHARA LEONIS.

There was nothing, of course. So she started trying variants of the name: DARA, DARRA, DARHA, and so forth.

Nothing.

Searching for Dhara Leonis had become a routine— the hunt had somehow become reassuring even as the lack of results remained frustrating. Part of Merei's brain registered each failure to turn up anything new even as the rest of her mind drifted from thought to thought: what Zare might be up to, how to tackle a tricky V-SIS assignment, the need to re-register her jump-speeder and get it inspected, what her family would be eating for dinner.

With her mind drifting, Merei failed to react when she heard her father's footsteps in the hall outside. The database was still on her screen when Gandr Spanjaf entered the apartment and strolled up behind her, whistling a horrifying cheesy Corulag show tune.

"Whatcha working on, Mer Bear?" her father asked, and she smiled at his old pet name for her even as she hurriedly blanked her screen.

"Didn't mean to sneak up on you," Gandr said, rooting around in the kitchen cooler for one of the cans of fizzy Moogan tea he loved. "What database were you looking at?"

"Um, customs," Merei said. "It's for school—intrusion countermeasures class. I'm trying to understand how their data is structured so I can see how an attacker might mimic a valid query."

Gandr sat down at the table and held the can of fizzy tea against his forehead. His hair was black and shaggy, peppered with gray.

"That's a relief," he said as he opened the can. "It would be bad for the family business if you got caught snooping in an Imperial Security Bureau data vault."

Her father grinned and Merei forced herself to smile back as he took a gulp of tea.

"And so how is the data structured over at Customs?" Gandr asked.

"Oh, Dad, I know you don't want to talk about this— it's what you do all day."

"Go ahead, try me."

Her father's eyes were bright above the can of tea. Merei hesitated, then rushed ahead.

"I think it would be easier if I just told you about the assignment I'm struggling with."

"You're probably right," Gandr said with a grin. "But I'm not doing your homework for you."

"I know. So I'm . . . well, I'm investigating a break-in launched by intruders who already had low-level access to a network—internal stuff, but nothing really sensitive. They managed to turn that into deeper access, but I'm not sure how."

Merei waited for Gandr's brow to wrinkle in suspicion. At least it was her father. Her mother would have leaned forward and started asking questions, and within a few minutes Merei would have been cornered by her own evasions. But Gandr just tossed the empty can into the recycler and smiled.

"Sounds kind of like the Imperial networks your mother and I are working on," he said, and Merei quickly stuffed her hands under her legs so he wouldn't see them flutter.

"When the Empire came to Lothal they were so concerned about putting systems in place fast that they didn't do a great job," Gandr said. "So now we've got teams tightening up security one ministry at a time. But it's slow going. For instance, we only sweep the networks for rogue programs and other breaches every other weekend, because the sweeps slow down network traffic so badly. But listen to me—you ask me about an intrusion and I go running off like a scalded nerf talking about sweep schedules."

"Oh, I didn't mind, Dad," Merei said. "That was interesting."

"But I didn't answer your question. There's all sorts of ways to get into a network, Mer Bear, but most security breaches are the fault of people, not systems. Nearly every really damaging intrusion I've seen was launched by someone who already had network access. But not because they were great slicers. The key was that they got into places where work was being done."

"You mean into the actual buildings themselves? The offices and ministries and places like that?"

"That's exactly what I mean," Gandr said.

"But isn't that much more dangerous than breaking in remotely? I mean, you'd get caught. The intruders, I mean. They'd get caught."

"You'd think so," Gandr said. "You'd think someone who saw a stranger doing something odd in their workplace would report it, or at least check their credentials. But that's not what happens. Most people assume strangers are who they say they are, particularly if they look and act the part. How did your intruders do what they did? Start by asking your teacher if someone traced the intrusion to its starting point. I bet it was within the network, and your intruder was a guy sitting at a desk who nobody thought to question."

The lowermost level at the Vocational School for Institutional Security was a maze of networking labs where students pursued all manner of projects: speeding up data traffic, structuring data for maximally efficient retrieval, and of course testing anti-intrusion protocols.

Merei checked her datapad again, then her position on the V-SIS floor plan, annoyed with herself that she still got lost at her own school.

This should be the lab I'm looking for, she thought, thumbing the door control.

"Whoa!" a voice called out in protest. "Bright light! Very bright light!"

Mumbling an apology, Merei hurried inside and found herself in a gloomy room full of network terminals and datapads connected by a crazy tangle of cables, some pulsing softly with light. Atop the desks, stacks of data cards fought for space with pyramids of old caf cans and discarded snack cartons.

Seven heads poked up from behind their terminals to peer at her. Most were human or near-human males, though she spotted a horned Gotal and a Bith she thought might have been female. They had tattoos and goatees and hair colored supernatural shades. All were wearing goggles and headsets.

"Welcome to our kingdom," a blue-skinned Pantoran boy proclaimed. "Now who are you and what do you want?"

"I'm Merei. Merei Spanjaf. I'm interested in intrusion countermeasures."

Laughter filled the cramped room.

"Of course you are," the Gotal said, whinnying in amusement. "You want to know how to break into networks so you can stop the bad guys and make the Empire a better place."

"Is there any other reason to break into a network?" asked a teenaged human with hair arranged into fearsome spikes.

"I can't think of one," the Pantoran replied, winking at Merei.

"I don't want to break into networks, for any reason," Merei said. "I'm looking for how to collect information from a network you're already inside."

The V-SIS students exchanged amused glances.

"Purely to monitor traffic patterns, right?" the Bith girl asked. "Not to, say, intercept messages and obtain access codes."

"Of course not," Merei said, offering what she hoped

was a devil-may-care shrug. "That would be wrong."

"I've never seen you down here before," a tall, thin boy wearing infochant's goggles said from the back. "New student?"

Merei nodded and the boy scoffed.

"You're a first year, and you want to intercept network traffic," he said, flicking his fingers at her dismissively. "Let me give you some advice, sister—you wanna see the spice mines of Kessel, get a tourist visa. It's less permanent than a detention cell. Now come back in a year or two when maybe you'll know what you're doing."

The students bent back over their terminals and datapads as if Merei were a hologram that had finished delivering its message. She looked around the gloomy room for a few seconds in frustration, then turned and hurried out.

"HEY! SPAMJACK!"

Merei killed her jumpspeeder's engine and raised her goggles, puzzled. The Pantoran boy from the computer lab was hurrying across the V-SIS lawn toward her, looking not entirely happy with being beneath the warm Lothal sun.

"Spamjack, wait."

"It's Spanjaf," she said. "Merei Spanjaf."

"Merei," the boy said as he came to a halt, breathing

hard. "Sorry about what happened back there. The other guys like to play a little rough, you know what I'm saying? But they don't really mean it."

"I'm pretty sure they did," Merei said.

"Well, I didn't," the boy said. He looked away, his cheeks flushing indigo.

"I'm Jix," he said. "Jix Hekyl. You were serious back there, weren't you?"

Merei nodded.

"Look, I'm not going to ask what you have in mind—that's so not my business," Jix said. "You're talking about a snooper—a program that records information and transmits it to an outside source. A basic one's pretty easy to configure, but you don't want a basic one—unless you don't care if someone finds it."

"I think I care about that," Merei said drily.

Jix grinned. "I think you do, too. What you need is something that won't throw off the traffic flow or do anything else that will get noticed. That's not so easy to program."

"I know my way around a terminal," Merei said.

"I'm not trying to insult you, Merei," Jix said hastily. "I'm saying I wouldn't do it. It's tricky. And illegal."

Neither of them said anything for a moment.

"How important is this to you?" Jix asked.

"Very," Merei said.

Jix sighed.

"I was afraid you'd say that. Look, I've done some programming work now and then—stuff I can't put on my school transcript, you know what I mean? I know a guy who knows a guy who maybe could help you with it. But that kind of help doesn't come cheap, or without strings attached."

"I understand," Merei said.

"I really hope you do," Jix said. "This is heavy firepower you're talking about, Merei."

"Good. Because that's what I need."

When Merei got home she commed the Leonises. After two chimes, the screen lit up, filled by the angular, copper-colored face of Auntie Nags, the family's ancient nanny droid.

"Merei Spanjaf, what a pleasure!" Auntie Nags said, her photoreceptors turning a cool green.

"Hello, Auntie," Merei said. "Is Tepha there?"

Auntie Nags's photoreceptors flared yellow. "Let me see if *Mrs. Leonis* is available," she said, turning away from the screen.

"She told me to call her Tepha, you know!" Merei said as the old droid rolled away.

Tepha Leonis appeared on the comm. She smiled at Merei, but there were deep hollows beneath her eyes.

"Merei! How are you? How's the new school?"

"I'm figuring it out," Merei said. "I wish I knew how Zare was doing, though."

"So do I," Tepha said with a sigh. She raised a mug to her lips, and Merei saw her nails were jagged and bitten.

"Have you heard anything new?" Merei asked.

Tepha looked off to the side, and Merei understood that Zare's father, Leo, was in the room—Leo, who didn't know that the Empire was lying about Dhara, or the real reason Zare had entered the Academy.

"Commandant Aresko's assistant commed two days ago," Tepha said. "He assured us the Empire is monitoring every channel in case Dhara turns up."

"I haven't heard anything either," Merei said. "But I have a feeling that will change soon."

Tepha's eyes widened with concern. She blinked hurriedly, then tried to smile.

"Well, we all hope so, Merei," she said, looking over at Leo before leaning closer to the comm.

Be careful, she mouthed.

Merei nodded. *I will.*

First came the helmets and harnesses, issued to each cadet at dawn by Currahee with orders to know every function backward and forward by the next day. The white cadet helmet was a variant of that worn in the Imperial Army, with a retractable faceplate that looked like a stormtrooper's, down to the frowning speaker grille.

Zare stared into the blank polarized lenses. The idea of putting the helmet on frightened him all of a sudden, as if he might never be able to remove it.

Oleg was standing atop his bunk, helmet on, pantomiming firing laser pistols at imagined enemies. Pandak was slumped against the wall, morosely trying to untangle his harness with his helmet at his feet.

"Cadet Oleg, ready to save the galaxy from Separatist scum," Jai said with a grin, poking at the innards of his helmet and then peering at the manual that had been automatically loaded on their datapads. "Say, Zare, is this the atmosphere intake or the suit air intake?"

"What does it matter?" Oleg asked, his voice filtered by the helmet's microphone. "Nothing's hooked up to anything."

"I bet it will matter to Curry," Zare said, peering at his own datapad. "Atmosphere intake's on the left, Jai. Suit air's on the right."

"Gotcha. Wait—my left or your left?"

"Your left—my right," Zare said, cycling his helmet's

vision processors from infrared to smoke filter and then to maximum polarization.

"Got it," said Jai's voice, now modulated by his own helmet.

Zare looked at his fellow cadets, their faces replaced by Imperial masks. He forced himself to raise the helmet above his head and slide it over his hair, then his eyes and ears. He hesitated, then closed the faceplate.

I wonder if Ames didn't want to put his on at first either.

The cadets were instructed to wear their helmets except on breaks, then marched across the Academy for their first day of classroom instruction. The cadets who couldn't figure out how to operate their audio pickups struggled miserably as Chiron and a succession of gray-haired instructors lectured them about operating as a squad, clearing hostile territory, and ballistics.

"If I wanted to study math I'd have stayed home," Oleg muttered to Zare.

Chiron turned from the parabola he was explaining, one eyebrow arched.

"Lesson one, Cadet Oleg: you can whisper, but the speakers in your bucket have no volume setting. That's a demerit."

Despite rumors to the contrary in the mess hall, the

cadets weren't ordered to sleep in their helmets, and Zare sighed gratefully as he finally removed his before hitting the shower. But they wore them again the next day, which began with every cadet issued an E-11 blaster rifle and told to take it apart, then put it back together—the first of a dozen such orders. By lights-out Zare's hands were cramped and he dreamed of nothing but blaster rifles, all of which turned out to be missing the trigger assembly or power cell that could have saved his life.

The day after that, they had to take their rifles apart and put them back together blindfolded. Then they donned their helmets and marched to the classroom.

The next morning, when Currahee burst in before dawn screaming for everyone to get in line, Zare wasn't surprised but simply dropped to the floor, reached for the crisply folded uniform atop his footlocker, and began to dress. Currahee's eyes flicked over him as he stood beside Jai, their chins raised, helmets against their hips under their left arms.

"Tolerable, Unit Aurek," she said grudgingly. "Now fall out—our troopship is waiting."

Troopship? Zare risked a glance at Jai, who shrugged.

Minutes later, the cadets rushed to the hangar, where Chiron was waiting in front of a landing ship, its triangular wings raised. A row of backpacks stood in front of them.

"A *Sentinel* class—wizard," Jai murmured as the cadets grabbed their packs and raced up the ramp to take seats on the benches in the troop compartment. When the last squad was aboard, Chiron and Currahee strode up the ramp, grabbing handholds as the hatch sealed behind them.

"Buckets off, cadets!" Chiron yelled. "Inside each pack you'll find a pauldron with a neck seal. Put it on and buckle the leads to the corresponding ports on your field pack, then put on your bucket. Make sure your neck seal is tight, or you'll regret it."

The deck of the landing ship began to thrum beneath their boots. The whine of the engines rose to a howl and then the cadets felt the ship lift off. A couple of cadets from the all-female Unit Forn cheered, earning a savage dressing-down from Currahee.

"Do you think we're going into space?" Pandak asked, and Zare could hear the nervousness even in his filtered voice.

"Not without environment suits, you fool," Oleg said. "They don't want to kill us during training. Though in your case it would be a good idea."

"Cadets!" yelled Chiron. "Switch your intakes to suit air!"

Zare made the switch as directed, suddenly glad for all the recent practice. He tapped at his atmosphere intake to make sure it was sealed, then elbowed Pandak to make sure he did the same.

The hatch opened and wind tore at the cadets. Chiron put one hand on his cap. Outside it was dark.

"Unit Aurek, assemble!" Currahee yelled, and Zare and the others scrambled to their feet.

"Move it, cadets!" Currahee shouted. "Jump! Your rendezvous point is due east!"

Oleg was first, and Zare saw him hesitate as he peered into the darkness around them. Before Currahee could yell he leapt out of the ship. Zare felt his legs shaking as he stood in the hatch, the wind whipping at his uniform.

"LEONIS! GO!"

Zare flung himself out of the *Sentinel* and tumbled through the sky. Impact jolted the air out of his lungs and he heard a splash. He was in the water, he realized—and sinking, weighed down by the heavy pack.

Do something!

He drew in a mouthful of suit air and began to kick. Everything around him was dark. He engaged his low-light filter and continued kicking, grunting with the effort, then broke the surface of the water. Where was everybody else?

He turned his comlink on and selected the channel reserved for his unit.

"Jai! Pandak! Oleg! Acknowledge!"

"It's Jai. Quite the wake-up call, huh, Zare?"

"Yep," Zare said. "Pandak? Oleg?"

"Already headed for the shore," Oleg said. "See if you slugs can keep up."

Scowling, Zare activated his helmet's compass and kicked until his head was pointed east. He switched to his infrared filter and saw a red blob that had to be Oleg ahead of him.

"Wait, Oleg—we advance as a unit, remember? Pandak?"

"I'm here," said Pandak. "Couldn't find the comlink controls. But I've got it now."

A few minutes later Zare felt mud and rocks beneath his feet and exhaled gratefully. The sun was just peeking over the horizon. Seatroopers in white armor were standing in the shallows of the lake, waiting to retrieve any cadets who sank or had problems with their air supplies.

They're not actively trying to kill us, Zare thought. *That's something.*

His comlink buzzed.

"I'm sending the next rendezvous point to your helmet navigation system," Chiron said. "It's ten klicks to the southeast. Arrive with your E-11 assembled and await further orders. Countdown begins now."

"Zare! We only have an hour," Jai said. "And nobody gave me an E-11."

Zare detached his pack and rummaged inside. "The rifles are in our packs—in pieces," he said. "We'll have to put them together while we run. Come on!"

Pandak was doing a good job of keeping up, Zare saw with relief, but he had to help him through two of the trickier aspects of assembling his E-11—and ignore Oleg, squawking impatiently over their comlinks for Zare to leave the other cadet behind.

"We're almost to the rendezvous, Pandak," Zare said. "Test your blaster—make sure it's drawing from the power pack."

Pandak fumbled with the rifle, gasping over the comlink.

"Indicator's green," he said. "Thanks, Zare."

"No worries," Zare said as they reached the knot of cadets and officers waiting at the rendezvous point. Jai gave them a jaunty salute, while Oleg waited with his arms crossed over his chest. A dozen other cadets sprawled dejectedly in the grass by the roadway, reassembling their rifles.

"LEONIS! SYMES!" Currahee said. "HAND OVER THOSE RIFLES!"

She glanced at Zare's power pack, thumbed the

safety on and off, then pointed the rifle at the roadway and pulled the trigger. A white bolt of energy struck sparks from the roadway.

"Very well, Leonis," she said, extending her hand for Pandak's rifle and firing another bolt into the pavement, then inclining her head toward Oleg and Jai. "You two join your squad."

"You only made it by five minutes," Oleg said. "You endangered our mission by playing babysitter."

"We had time, Oleg," Zare said. "We're stronger with four—when are you going to learn that?"

"About the same time you figure out that depends on the four," Oleg said.

A chime sounded over the cadets' comlinks—the hour was up. Currahee stood in the roadway, waiting to intercept the cadets who hadn't finished yet, while Chiron yelled for the others to gather around him, with the boys and girls who hadn't assembled their rifles correctly watching resentfully.

"Buckets off and listen up," Chiron said.

Zare pulled his helmet off gratefully, rubbing his forehead on the sleeve of his uniform. Jai had his hands on his knees, E-11 and helmet in the grass at his feet.

"Ahead of you is an obstacle course—each unit has a goal, the location of which will be loaded into your helmets. If your unit's below full strength, you'll just have to do the best you can. The course features broken terrain, and it's defended by Imperial troops—don't worry, today their blasters are on training setting. Get hit and you're out. Form up by unit, select a leader, and move out on my mark. You'll have ten minutes to reach your objective."

"I'm the leader," Oleg said as they walked up a path to the start of the obstacle course.

"Says who?" asked Jai. "Zare should lead."

"Don't be ridiculous—"

"I vote for Zare," Pandak said.

Oleg scowled, then reached for his helmet.

"Whatever," he said.

"Wait, Oleg, I haven't voted yet," Zare said. "It could still be a tie."

The other three looked at him.

"Really?" Oleg asked.

Zare shook his head. "Of course not. I'm unit leader."

He put on his helmet and scanned the area ahead of them. It was a grassy field broken up by clumps of rock and boulders.

A chime in their ears signaled the start of the exercise. Cadets began moving in threes and fours across the field. There was no sign of the trainers awaiting them.

"Let's move out," Zare said, thinking back to the

classroom demonstrations. "Wedge formation, but be ready to shift to file formation at the chokepoints. I'm point. Pandak, you're on my left. Oleg and Jai, on my right."

"I see the goal," Oleg said. "Keep up a field of fire and I can get there before you three get taken out."

"Back in line," Zare said. "We'll do it together. Now come on."

They crept into the field, bent low over their E-11s. Ahead of them Zare could hear the sizzle of blaster bolts and cadets yelling. A trainer in a gray uniform popped up and they dove into the grass as a brilliant bolt illuminated their hiding place.

"Spread out," Zare said. "Pandak, go left and attract his attention. Oleg, Jai, move right to encircle him."

Not so different than the grav-ball grid, he thought, smiling.

The other cadets crept away through the grass. Pandak popped up, firing his E-11 wildly. Oleg and Jai dashed forward, crouched low, as Zare moved forward on his knees, cycling his helmet to infrared and cranking his helmet's audio inputs as high as they would go.

A branch snapped ahead of Zare and he froze.

"Pandak, down—he's got your position," he said over the comlink. "Oleg, Jai, come in from the right. Stay low, but make noise."

He heard the movement on his right and crept forward on his hands and knees. He could see a faint red haze ahead of him. Something rustled in the grass and Zare sprang forward, blaster raised. The trainer turned, but Zare's blaster bolt caught him in the chest before he could raise his rifle.

"Ow," he said, getting to his feet. "I forgot how much that stings. Nice job, kid."

"Thank you, sir," Zare said. "Aurek, reorient on the objective."

Other cadets were walking back through the grass now, heads down, out of the competition. Unit Aurek moved forward in pairs until the goal was twenty meters ahead. Zare peeked above a mossy hillock and saw the ground rose gradually ahead of them.

"They'll have the high ground," he said. "And they have a better vantage point. Switch to file formation— we've got to cross that open space, then we'll look to flank them. Got it?"

"It's a dumb plan," Oleg muttered.

"Your objection is noted, cadet," Zare said. "Now let's go. I'll take lead. Then Jai, Pandak, and Oleg."

They crept forward without meeting opposition. Zare held his hand up, signaling for the others to wait. His eyes scanned the open field ahead of them, then jumped to the boulders and low hills that dotted it. How many places were there where an attacker could hide? Five? Six?

There was no way around it, he thought.

"Low and fast to that little clump of shrubs," Zare said. "When we get there, fire team wedge, overlapping coverage. Let's go!"

He was halfway across the open space when the first trainer popped up to his right, sending a blaster bolt zinging past his ear. Zare squeezed off a few hasty shots, stumbled, and just missed catching a bolt from the trainer concealed to his left. He dropped his E-11, scooped it up, and fell into the bushes, branches scraping across his helmet.

The rest of Unit Aurek crashed down around him.

"Pandak, cover the rear flank," Zare said. "Anybody hit?"

"We're here, aren't we?" grumbled Oleg.

"Good," Zare said. "I saw two on the left, but only one on the right. Make for that reddish rock over there. Wedge formation—Oleg, Jai, you make sure the guy on the right keeps his head down. Pandak, left side is your responsibility."

"This isn't going to work," Oleg said.

"Sure it will," Zare said. "In grav-ball we call it a weak-side carry—I won a league championship with this play."

"We've got three minutes left, Zare," Jai said.

"Plenty of time," Zare said, though of course in this game you couldn't call a time-out. "Let's go."

He started forward, with Oleg on his right. They'd gone three meters when Jai yelled his name.

"Down!" Zare said. "What is it?"

"It's Pandak," Jai said. "He's not moving."

"What? Is he hurt?"

Zare scrambled back and found Pandak crouched behind the clump of bushes. He had taken his helmet off and his eyes were wide and staring.

"Hey, Pandak," Zare said. "We've got to go, cadet."

"They're going to get us," Pandak said. "They're going to get us. Going to get us going to get us going to get us."

"No, they're not," Zare said. "Put your bucket on and stick with me."

"Zare, two minutes," Jai said.

"Come on, Pandak," Zare pleaded.

"Forget this—we're going," Oleg said.

"Hold your position," Zare said.

"Going to get us," Pandak said, hugging his helmet to his chest.

"Pandak, stay here," Zare said. "Jai, I'm coming."

He rushed forward as blaster bolts erupted around him from the left and right. He wound up sprawled next to Oleg and Jai.

"We're not gonna make it," Jai moaned.

"Yes, we are," Zare said. "Were you watching when I ran? Where did the shots come from?"

"Five meters to the right," Oleg said. "And two firing positions to the left. Six meters and maybe seven."

"All right," Zare said. "File position to the right, at the enemy, fast as you can. I'll break left, you flank to the right. GO!"

He'd gone three meters, firing wildly, before something struck him in the back and he stumbled, his skin on fire.

"Blast it," he muttered, raising his hands. But then he heard firing ahead of him, and a glum-faced trainer rose up from behind a bush. Jai and Oleg whooped in triumph, their yells dissolving into static in his ears, as the chime sounded the end of the exercise.

Zare sank into the seat in Chiron's office, wanting nothing more than to get to his bunk and sleep.

"We monitor all the unit feeds during exercises," Chiron said. "You showed initiative, kept your unit together, and improvised when things went wrong. That was real leadership out there."

"I got killed," Zare said.

"You secured the objective. And if Symes hadn't

frozen up, you would have had covering fire to your rear during that flanking maneuver."

"Pandak will do better next time," Zare said. "I can help him."

Chiron looked at the ceiling, the corners of his mouth turned down.

"An Imperial soldier can't quit under fire," he said. "It endangers more than one life. You saw that for yourself today."

"But, sir—"

"You were center striker for AppSci, Zare," Chiron said. "How many victories would you have had if one of your fullbacks froze when you told him to block?"

Zare started to object, then just nodded glumly.

"All right then," Chiron said. "Now go get some sleep."

He trudged back to the barracks and found Oleg lying on Pandak's bunk, grinning. Jai was sitting numbly on his own bunk, feet dangling over the edge. Pandak's footlocker was gone.

PART 2:
IMPERSONATION

A couple of days of digging and carefully constructed questions at the dinner table gave Merei her target: the Transportation Ministry. It was connected to the entire Imperial network, heavily reliant on outside contractors instead of bureaucratic lifers, and way down on her parents' security to-do list.

The problem, she thought as she got on her jumpspeeder, was that she still hadn't worked out how to get into the ministry.

I'm only fifteen, she thought as she fitted her goggles over her eyes. *No one would believe I'm a contractor, or maintenance crew, or anything else.*

She shivered at the chill—this was the first morning it felt like autumn, which meant the grasslands would soon be turning pale green and brown. And in the hills the jogan blossoms would be at their most fragrant—if

Beck Ollet were there, he'd be urging her to ride out to the orchardlands.

Then her smile faded away. Because Beck wasn't there—he was a prisoner of the Empire. And for all she knew there were no more jogan trees in the stripped and ruined hills.

At least I'll get to talk to Zare tonight, she thought as she maneuvered the jumpspeeder away from her parents' apartment house and into the sparse traffic. It was the last day of orientation, and after dinner the cadets would be allowed to comm their families and friends again.

And I'll have to tell him I'm no closer to finding Dhara, she thought, then shook her head. *Maybe the guy I'm going to meet can change that. Well, unless he's Imperial intelligence. What are the rules for cadets with girlfriends in jail?*

Merei zipped around a slow-moving droid truck, passing through the low-slung buildings of Old City, with their whitewashed stone walls and bright awnings. She reached the outskirts of the marketplace and parked her jumpspeeder, locking down the controls. The shops and stalls were crowded with humans, aliens, and droids making deliveries—green-skinned Rodians brushed shoulders with mournful-looking, whiskered Lutrillians, blocking the path of automated cargo loaders that beeped and hooted angrily.

She shouldered her way through the crowd, escaping a close encounter with a crate of juicemelons that two bald, quarreling Sakiyans swung into her path. There it was—the stall Jix's friend had told her about. The shutters were down almost all the way to the ground, but she saw a bit of dim light beneath them.

Merei knocked on the metal, producing a lot more noise than she'd expected. She stepped back, blushing, as heads turned around her.

A gnarled hand appeared and cranked the shutter up, revealing a short, wizened human with a gray topknot. He looked her up and down quizzically, then spat on the floor.

"Um . . . Bandis Yong sent me," Merei said.

"Who in the name of the Great Prairie Winds is Bandis Yong and why should I care?"

"He graduated from the Vocational School for Institutional Security a couple of years ago. He said you could help me."

"He told you wrong—now get lost," the old man said, then leaned closer. "Duck under the shutter in five minutes. And this time, try to make less noise than a walker falling off a cliff."

Merei stopped herself from nodding and stalked off in what she hoped looked like a huff. She made a circuit of the market, glancing idly at rainbows of fruit, slabs of meat, and repaired machinery that supposedly worked even better than it had before. She stopped in front of the stall again, looked around, and then got down on her knees, worming under the metal shutter.

The old man turned from a cluttered desk in the corner of the stall topped with an ancient network terminal.

"Bandis Yong," he said. "Young punk with delusions of being a master slicer. A rude and talentless cretin. That him?"

"Pretty much," Merei said, wiping grit on her trousers. Bandis Yong's inflated self-regard had been matched only by his hygiene problems, and he'd asked her out no fewer than three times, ignoring Merei's insistence that she wasn't interested and only giving up the sixth time she said she had a boyfriend.

"So what do you need from me, girlie? Besides better taste in friends?"

"An introduction," Merei said. She took a deep breath. "To someone who can program a snooper for me."

The old man laughed, the sound a harsh bark.

"Sun's barely up and a skinny girl with expensive

bike goggles and a Core accent wants me to introduce her to someone who'll make a snooper for her," the old man said, putting his skinny wrists together and holding them out in front of him. "Here—just put the binders on and comm Governor Pryce to send over some stormtroopers. It would save us all time."

He laughed again, waving a hand at her in dismissal.

"Get lost, girlie. And don't come back."

Merei turned to go, then shook her head and leaned against the shutters, the metal groaning in protest.

"I'm not leaving until you help me," she said.

"Feel free to wait," the old man said, sitting down at his terminal. "Lothal's sun won't go nova for a few billion years."

"*Please*," Merei said. "I've got nowhere else to go."

The old man looked over his shoulder.

"What part of 'get lost' didn't you understand?" he asked. But he couldn't meet her eyes.

Merei waited.

"I'm going to regret this," he muttered. "Be at the East Interchange where it intersects Founders' Avenue tomorrow at dawn. An unmarked speeder van will pull up. You'll get in. After that it's up to you."

"That sounds like an excellent way to disappear," Merei said, but the old man just shrugged.

"Not my problem, girlie," he said. "You want to do business, you'll be there."

Merei nodded and scuttled back under the door into the marketplace, now bustling with morning shoppers. She dodged household droids, passed a line of fidgety bureaucrats waiting to spend too many credits for artisanal caf, and was almost back to her jumpspeeder when two girls a couple of years younger than she stepped in front of her.

"Hi," one of them said breathlessly. "We're selling raffle tickets to raise funds for our Junior Academy camping trip in the Westhills. Would you like to buy one? It's for a good cause and a ticket is only one credit."

"No thanks," Merei said, stepping around the girls. Then she stopped. "Wait. What did you say?"

The moment he saw his mother's face on the screen, Zare felt his composure slip, then crumble. To his embarrassment, his eyes welled up and tears began to roll down his cheeks.

"We're glad to see you, too, son," Leo Leonis said gruffly from where he stood behind Tepha. "So how are you getting along at the Academy?"

Zare wiped his eyes on his sleeve and took a deep breath, reminding himself not to be upset with his father. Leo had been devastated by Dhara's disappearance, but Zare and Tepha hadn't told him that they knew the Empire was lying, and that its attempts to find her were a sham. He didn't know that his son was risking the same fate.

Tepha did know all that, of course, and it was the relief on his mother's face that got to Zare—the way her eyes widened when she saw him on the other side of the video link, and the shuddering breath she took before saying his name.

"I'm fine," he said hastily. "Glad orientation's over, of course, but fine. I'm looking forward to seeing you guys at Visiting Day."

"Have they given you any sense of which track you'll be on?" Leo asked.

"It's too early, Dad," Zare said. "They haven't said anything, but based on what Dhara told me last year, we should start assessments next week."

His sister's name stopped conversation cold. Leo blinked furiously, then forced himself to nod, while Tepha buried her face in her hands. Leo put his hand on his wife's shoulder.

"Sorry," Zare said.

"You have nothing to be sorry about, son," Leo said. "The Empire is working every day to find Dhara and see that she returns home. You just focus on being the best cadet you can be, and leave worrying about your sister to others."

"I will, Dad," Zare said. "Um, I have to go."

His mother put her hand on the camera and Zare reached for his own datapad, pressing his palm against the glass.

He needed a moment to get himself together before comming Merei. They talked about anything and everything—V-SIS, the Academy, the cold snap that had settled over Capital City—interrupting each other and stopping and insisting the other say what they were going to say, then laughing helplessly and starting again, until finally they just looked at each other, smiling.

Zare sighed, and then leaned close to his datapad.

"I haven't heard anything from our friend about her trip," he said. "Nothing about where she is or who she might be with. Have you heard anything?"

Merei shook her head. "No. But keep your chin up, Zare. I've got some ideas about how I might find something out."

Zare nodded. "Good. Thank you. But . . . don't get in trouble, okay, Merei?"

His girlfriend smiled. "I was about to tell you the same thing."

★ ★ ★

"CADETS! INSPECTION IS IN TEN MINUTES!"

Zare barely even grumbled as he dropped out of his bunk to stand next to Jai, with Oleg getting to his feet opposite them a moment later. He pulled his footlocker out from under Jai's bunk and retrieved his uniform, stripping off the T-shirt he'd slept in.

Eight minutes later he was dressed and next to Jai, waiting for Currahee to return. He saw Oleg throw his shoulders back and raise his chin and did the same as the sergeant entered the barracks, staring malevolently at the cadets. She stopped in front of Zare and eyed his uniform, then his boots. Then she inspected his helmet minutely, followed by his E-11. She grunted and peered at his bunk, having to stand on her tiptoes to do so. Behind her back, Oleg smirked. Zare didn't move; he remained at attention, staring at Oleg as Currahee repeated the process with Jai and then Oleg. Zare knew his bunk was perfectly made, his uniform was crisp and clean, his boots were shined as specified by regulations, and his helmet and E-11 were in working order.

"Well done, Unit Aurek," Currahee said. "You might have a future as cadets after all. Now fall out—we're going on a morning run."

Once the cadets would have groaned in dismay, but now the prospect of toiling up and down the Easthills was barely worthy of notice.

"We did it!" Jai said in a low voice, beaming as Currahee moved on to yell at Unit Besh. "Not one demerit!"

Zare smiled back, then turned away, a shiver running through him. *What am I doing? Who cares about that old hawk-bat's approval? Curry's a servant of the Empire—the same Empire that stole my sister, that's killed peaceful protestors, and is ruining Lothal.*

He couldn't allow himself to be fooled by praise from Currahee, or Chiron's efforts to help him, or by becoming friends with cadets such as Jai. He had to remember what happened to Dhara, and stay alert to avoid the same fate.

The upper-crust Phelarion School was reserved for the sons and daughters of Capital City's top Imperial officials, wealthy merchants, farming tycoons, and minerals magnates. Its home data node showed an attractive teenage boy and girl in black uniforms. To one side were lush green fields and conical hills like those of Lothal; to the other, gleaming urban towers.

The students were facing the towers—*turning their backs on Lothal*, Merei thought with a smile.

She didn't even have to break into the school's network to find a roster of students—she was able to guess the address of the correct data node on the third try.

Merei scanned the roster quickly, searching for a girl about her age with Imperial connections—high, but not too high.

A network search revealed her first target was the daughter of a local swoop jockey from beyond the Westhills who'd taken his winnings and invested them in a fertilizer company.

Too low.

Her second target had a last name that seemed familiar—and turned out to be the youngest daughter of a lieutenant colonel in the Imperial Army.

Too high.

Plexo-33 began warbling on her datapad. She killed the music feed irritably. She had to get moving if she was going to keep her rendezvous. Her parents thought she was headed for a club meeting with some V-SIS students interested in anti-intrusion techniques, but she actually planned to meet the unmarked speeder van on the outskirts of Capital City.

Which is probably a terrible idea.

She had time to try another name or two. She scanned the list of birthdates, then tapped the screen.

Hello, Kinera Tiree—who are you?

A quick search revealed that Kinera Tiree was the

daughter of the Imperial education minister on Lothal.

Just right, Merei thought as she blanked her screen.

The speeder van was white, but so covered with dirt and dents that its color was all but undetectable. It slowed with a whine of poorly tuned repulsorlifts, stopping alongside Merei where she sat astride her jumpspeeder outside an abandoned repair shop whose holograph sign kept spitting out sad little blurs of color.

The driver was a mustachioed alien of a species she didn't know, with five eyes arranged in an X and hidden behind mirrored lenses.

"Get in back," it rumbled.

"What about my jumpspeeder?" Merei asked.

"Leave it."

"In this neighborhood?"

"Lock it up, then. You've got one minute. Things go right, someone will bring you back."

"And if things go wrong?"

The alien shrugged and laughed, revealing a throat filled with wicked, inward-pointing spines.

Merei locked up her jumpspeeder and the alien inclined its head toward the back of the van. The doors opened to reveal a pair of grubby-looking human males and a Rodian female whose mane of crimson spikes made for a bizarre contrast with her green skin. Merei hesitated, then scrambled up into the van. The doors slammed shut and the van took off almost immediately. Merei stumbled and the Rodian grabbed her.

"Search her," she said in a honking voice.

The men's hands were rough and impersonal. The trio just laughed when Merei glared at them. Then they aimed a handheld scanner at her, telling her to turn around.

"She's clean, boss," one of them said.

"Might have a hidden transmitter, though," said the other. "Saw that in a gang war on Tirahnn. Want me to open up her skull and check? It just makes a little hole."

They're just trying to scare you, Merei told herself, crossing her arms and taking a seat on a bench against the wall. The men and the Rodian laughed, then ignored her as the van stopped and started, turning left and right in rapid succession.

After a few minutes the van eased to a halt, settling on its repulsorlifts with a sigh. The Rodian opened the back of the van and indicated for Merei to go first. She found herself in an alley choked with trash, its mouth blocked by the speeder van. Halfway down, the Rodian rapped on a metal door. Inside was a filthy kitchen where a burly Aqualish leaned against the cooktop, cleaning a blaster pistol. He exchanged nods with the Rodian, who shoved Merei in the back.

Beyond the kitchen was a dilapidated tavern dominated by an L-shaped bar, its countertop lined with network terminals. A motley collection of young humans and aliens looked up at Merei curiously, then returned to their keyboards. The ceiling was patched and marred by long streaks of soot. Blackout curtains covered the windows, and thugs of various species sat in little groups at the mismatched tables and chairs.

The Rodian murmured into her comlink, then wrinkled her snout in annoyance.

"The boss says you got two minutes. This way."

Merei stumbled over a deep gouge in the floor as she trailed the Rodian through the back room and up a narrow flight of stairs to a door. It opened and the Rodian shoved Merei inside. A large window missing its glass overlooked an anonymous street that might have been anywhere in Old City. Three porcine Ugnaughts were taking turns measuring the frame, squealing and jabbing knobby fingers at one another.

"So you're the schoolgirl whose hobby is snoopers," said a booming voice. It belonged to a heavyset man sitting in the corner behind an Imperial officer's desk. His network terminal was glossy black and state of the art.

"That's right," Merei said neutrally as the Rodian

settled herself onto a nerfhide couch that was losing its stuffing, one hand near the blaster pistol strapped to her hip.

"And if for some reason I agreed to supply such a program, what specifications would it have?"

"Archive of logged keystrokes, ability to monitor and record traffic across all network channels, transmission to an external node according to my specifications, keystroke/traffic logs encrypted using a key I'd supply, and a built-in self-destruct that erases the snooper from the active node and any archives after a time period I set."

The man behind the desk chuckled. He had a preposterous blond pompadour and blue eyes that were bright with intelligence.

"Is that all? You don't need a spare military droid brain to generate tactical recommendations for a sector fleet? Or the services of Emperor Palpatine's top infochant?"

"Not at the moment," Merei said. "If things change, I'll let you know."

"I bet you will," the man said, struggling to lift his feet onto the desk. He was wearing lilac bedroom slippers, Merei noted with amusement. "What you're asking for isn't cheap. You better not be wasting my time."

"I've got the credits," Merei said.

"Glad to hear it. Time we were formally introduced. I'm Yahenna Laxo. And you're in the new headquarters of the Gray Syndicate."

That seemed a bit much for a bunch of slicers barely out of V-SIS and a handful of Old City thugs, but Merei limited herself to a nod and the faintest hint of a smirk.

Laxo saw it anyway.

"Vizago himself has used our services," he rumbled, eyes narrowing in anger. "We know everything that happens in Capital City. Such as the fact that you're Merei Spanjaf, freshwoman at V-SIS, recent immigrant from Corulag, and now, it seems, an apprentice criminal. That would come as a surprise to the Imperial network contractors you call Mom and Dad."

Merei's mouth was suddenly very dry.

"What's the matter, kid, Loth-cat got your tongue? Don't look so surprised—no way I was letting you get within a kilometer of my shop without knowing who you are. What I can't figure out, Merei Spanjaf, is why you're here and what you want with a snooper. Care to enlighten me?"

"No," Merei said. "There aren't enough credits on Lothal for me to tell you that."

Laxo laughed long and loud, putting his hands on his belly. The Ugnaughts looked up from their work and squealed at each other in puzzlement, then shrugged.

"I like you, kid," Laxo said. "I know Rosey thinks I shouldn't—she keeps hoping I'll tell her to shoot you—but I do. Keep your secrets, Merei Spanjaf, but if I'm going to help you, you have to do something for me. I've got a package I need brought to someone at the marketplace."

"What kind of package?" Merei asked, thinking Laxo didn't have to shoot her to get rid of her—he could do that just as effectively, and more safely, by setting her up to be found carrying something illegal.

"There aren't enough credits on Lothal for me to tell you that," Laxo said with a grin. "When you leave I'll get on the comm. Hand the package over as instructed and you'll get a drive containing the code for your snooper."

Merei heard Rosey get up from the couch behind her. She scowled, but didn't see an alternative to helping Laxo.

"All right," she said, turning so quickly that Rosey took an involuntary step backward, skin flushing a darker green with annoyance. "Let's get moving, then."

"Glad to have you working for me," Laxo said with a grin.

"I don't work for you," Merei said.

"We'll see about that," Laxo said as the door shut behind her.

★ ★ ★

The cadets could tell from the moment Currahee began yelling that something special was happening—the squat sergeant was even louder than usual, and stopped to look each cadet in the eye where he or she stood in front of a bunk.

Currahee grunted and marched to the middle of the barracks, staring up and down the lines of cadets.

"You will assemble by units in the main hangar in ten minutes!" Currahee blared. "You will be wearing helmets! You will be wearing harnesses! You will be prepared for action!"

"About time we wore these things," Jai said. "Wonder what they're for?"

Zare just shook his head. Dhara had told him about many aspects of cadet life, from the dawn runs to security measures in Imperial headquarters, but she'd never mentioned the harnesses.

The cadets marched through the halls of the Academy and entered its massive main hangar. AT-DPs were arrayed on both sides of the huge chamber, their heads looking wobbly on their tall, spiderlike legs. The blast doors leading to the plaza outside the Academy were closed.

Zare double-checked the straps on his harness and lowered the faceplate on his helmet. A double line of stormtroopers entered the hall, their white armor glossy under the overhead lights. As the cadets elbowed each other, the troopers lined up on either side of the massed students.

Currahee and Chiron walked into the hall, faces serious. They halted in front of the cadets, who instinctively came to attention. Currahee walked up and down the lines, hands behind her back, and barked at cadets to shorten harness straps, attend to blemishes on their boots, and straighten cuffs and belts.

Satisfied, the sergeant rejoined Chiron. A section of the floor slid aside and the two officers saluted, the cadets hurriedly copying the motion. A platform rose into the air. Atop it, Zare recognized the lean, cadaverous figure of Commandant Aresko next to the broad bulk of his assistant, Grint.

The platform settled to the hangar floor and Aresko stepped off, followed by Grint. The commandant extended a black-gloved hand and Grint placed a datapad into it. Aresko glanced up and down between the datapad and the cadets.

"Welcome to the assessment hall," Aresko said. "All four of these squads are at less than full complement. Sergeant Currahee? What became of Cadet Illorus, Unit Forn?"

"Dismissed after second failure to achieve objectives during combat training, sir," Currahee said.

"I see," Aresko said. "And Cadet O'Harlan, Unit Esk?"

"Voluntary withdrawal at end of orientation, sir," Currahee said.

"Very well." Aresko continued up and down the lines of cadets, quizzing Currahee and Chiron about each missing member of the class, until he had returned to his platform.

"And Cadet Symes, Unit Aurek?"

"Voluntary withdrawal, sir."

Zare steeled himself not to look at Oleg.

"Winnowing out the unworthy is an essential part of the process of finding the best cadets to keep our Empire strong," Aresko said. "You have proven that you are those cadets—Lothal's best and brightest. Over the next couple of weeks, your units will be brought back to full strength through transfers from Lothal's other regional academies. But those cadets will find it is no easy task living up to the example you have set so far. My congratulations to you all. At ease, cadets."

The hangar erupted in noise as the cadets hugged, slapped palms, and cheered. Jai and Zare raised their faceplates, beaming, and shook hands. Caught up in the moment, Zare even gave Oleg an answering nod.

He regretted it immediately.

"A transfer cadet will be no competition," Oleg sneered. "Whoever he is, he won't have been through orientation like we have. We'll eat him alive."

"He'll be part of our unit, Oleg," Zare said. "That means we'll work together. *All* of us."

"Cadets! At attention!" Currahee blared.

Aresko and Grint's platform had risen some ten meters above the hangar floor.

"And now, cadets, the next phase of your training begins," Aresko said, his voice amplified. "Over the rest of the term you will undergo numerous assessments— designed to measure your physical prowess, mental acuity, leadership skills, and strategic adaptability."

The cadets remained rigid, staring at the platform above their heads.

"Many of these assessments will be conducted here—the floor beneath your boots can be remotely configured in any number of ways," Aresko said. "This facility is basic—progress far enough as servants of the Empire and one day you might see what a course on Raithal or even Carida is like. But it will suit our needs. Your first assessment begins . . . right now."

Currahee and Chiron herded the cadets into a ring, glancing back and forth from their feet to the floor. Jai and Zare looked at each other nervously. Zare lowered his faceplate and Jai did the same.

The floor inside the ring suddenly dropped away, becoming a pit lined with a grid of white light. Several cadets took involuntary steps backward. Zare saw Grint and Aresko exchange a smile. Platforms detached themselves from the walls of the pit, floating across on repulsorlifts before being reabsorbed by the opposite wall.

"This is the Well, cadets," Aresko said. "You'll come to know it intimately."

Zare leaned over to peer into the pit, but Jai tugged on the back of his harness. A moment later a Pillar rose from the bottom of the pit, thickening as it ascended to floor level. It nearly filled the ring of cadets as it rose, halting a meter above their heads. Zare looked at the surface of the Pillar and saw rings appear from its smooth sides—rings that began to blink a pale green.

"And this, cadets, is the Pillar. I'd suggest you find an attachment point."

Zare stepped forward and clipped the carabiner on his harness to the ring closest to him, holding on and bracing his feet against the Pillar where it intersected the floor. In ones and twos the other cadets did the same.

Suddenly the Pillar shot upward, carrying the cadets with it.

"Going up!" yelled Oleg where he clung to his ring next to Zare.

The Pillar stopped rising two meters shy of the hall's ceiling. Zare braced his feet against the side of the Pillar and risked a look down. The AT-DPs and the stormtroopers looked small from up there.

The platform occupied by Aresko and Grint floated near the top of the Pillar.

A chime sounded in Zare's helmet.

"Climb down, cadets," Aresko said calmly. "QUICKLY!"

Zare tried not to think of how far it was to the floor of the hall. He spotted a ring a meter below his feet to the right. He checked that his carabiner was firmly attached to the ring, released the lock on his primary belay loop, and rappelled down to the ring, onto which he locked his secondary belay loop's carabiner. He tugged at it to verify it was locked, then released the other carabiner.

Zare risked a look around. Several cadets were tugging at their harnesses, no doubt regretting having not spent more hours learning how they worked. A cadet from Unit Dorn slipped and fell and wound up dangling beneath his waist belt, kicking helplessly.

Zare, Jai, and Oleg began to descend, swinging back and forth in search of rings. As Zare searched, a platform emerged below his feet, while above him part of the Pillar retracted, forming a narrow rectangular cave.

Jai unlocked his carabiner and jumped two meters down, landing on a platform with a grunt—a risky maneuver, but one that gave him a lead in the race to the floor. He shook his head, momentarily dazed, and attached his line to a nearby ring just as the platform beneath him began to retract.

Zare and Oleg looked around and spotted a platform emerging below them. Zare unlocked his carabiner and dropped to the new surface, falling onto his butt and fumbling for a ring. Oleg landed beside him, slipped, and fell onto his face. Zare grabbed his harness's waist belt before he could tumble over the edge.

"Don't touch me, Leonis," Oleg growled, but Zare was already scanning for the next platform below them.

He reached the bottom and raised his faceplate, breathing hard. Jai grinned at him where he stood in a knot of other cadets. He held up three fingers.

"Sixth, Leonis," Currahee said.

A cadet from Unit Besh landed on the deck beside Zare, followed a moment later by Oleg. They moved aside as more cadets arrived, looking up at those hanging forlornly with no platform within reach. Then the chime signaling the end of the exercise sounded.

"At ease," Aresko said from above. "Winners are Cadets de Grom, Wheeler, and Kell. Well done. Each of you qualifies for an extra dessert ration and free period. The top three finishers in each assessment will receive rewards—including weekend passes and work details at Imperial headquarters. But as you've discovered today, earning these rewards will not be easy. You will have to find new levels of courage and ingenuity. I wish you good luck, cadets. Squads dismissed."

The cadets whooped, with two members of Unit Esk already arguing what to do with the weekend jaunt they'd win. But Zare was thinking only of Imperial headquarters. If he could get inside headquarters, perhaps he could discover what the Empire had done with Dhara.

Which meant he had to win those assessments.

"Mom! I'm home!"

Merei brought the bags into the kitchen, where her mother was chopping vegetables at the counter. She took out the prairie-fowl breasts and tubers and set them in front of Jessa, who looked them over and nodded approvingly. Then her mother's eyes jumped to the other bag over Merei's shoulder.

"What's the rest of that stuff?" she asked.

"Oh, just some things for school," Merei said offhandedly, hoping that would be enough for her mother. Gandr

Spanjaf could figure out the architecture of a network a sector away while not noticing something right in front of his face, but Jessa rarely missed anything, whether it was being two minutes late for curfew or the single typo in a school essay. She noticed things, which was bad, and she asked questions, which was worse.

Merei hurried up the stairs, only relaxing when she was far enough away to claim she hadn't heard her mother calling after her. She tossed the bag into the top of her closet, wondering what her mother would have thought if she'd seen Merei had bought three fingertip-sized network drives, a book of old-fashioned flimsi receipts, and a secondhand T-shirt from the Phelarion School.

Yes, Jessa Spanjaf would definitely have had some questions about that.

A series of commands gave her access to the private area of her datapad where she'd been testing the Gray Syndicate's snooper program. The snooper seemed to do everything she'd requested—she'd programmed it to record everything entered into the computer it was installed on, capture any data that passed through that computer, and send a log of that information to a remote location where she could retrieve it. Once activated, the snooper would work for the amount of time she requested, then delete itself from memory.

That was it, then, Merei thought. There were no tests left to run—she had to get the snooper onto the Imperial network.

Merei heard something and paused. Yes, that was definitely her mother calling to her—and she sounded annoyed. She hurried downstairs to the smell of roasting fowl.

"I have to watch the vegetables—the oven's gauge is acting up, and they'll burn. Set the table, please?"

"Sure," Merei said, eyeing the different stacks of plates. She held one up for her mother's inspection and Jessa nodded. But Merei could feel her mother's eyes remaining on her as she put out the plates.

"How are your courses at V-SIS?" Jessa asked.

"Fine," Merei said.

"Your dad says you've been working on anti-intrusion measures. Both at school and in some sort of club."

"That's right," Merei said.

"Well, that's a better use of your time than grav-ball or joyriding with boys," Jessa said.

It was an old fight, and Merei refused to take the bait. But she knew she'd have to volunteer something to avoid an interrogation.

"Anti-intrusion is interesting stuff," she said. "I like

it because it's not just figuring out how programs and networks work—it's about people, too."

"That's right," Jessa said. "No one has ever created a security protocol that can't be defeated by the wrong people's bad habits."

"So how do you use the security protocols to make them adopt good habits?"

"You can't, really," Jessa said. "I mean, you can make people change their access codes, but then they'll just write them on flimsi next to their terminals. Like I always say, you can't fix stupid. Let's test what you've learned—give me some measures you'd use to make a site's network more secure."

"Don't reuse access codes," Merei said as she repositioned the glasses. "Lock down your terminal any time you leave. Don't leave datapads, network drives, or decoders unattended. Don't install outside programs on the network. Ask people you don't know who they are and why they're there. Oh, and don't hold doors for people."

Jessa looked up from the oven and nodded.

"That last one's probably the most important," she said. "And how many of those things do you need a programmer for?"

"Well, you can disallow the installation of outside

programs," Merei said. "Other than that, you don't need a programmer for any of it."

"Actually it's even worse than that," Jessa said. "You can disallow installations, but then you need to pay some poor programmer to sit around doing stuff a half-blind Lurmen could manage. Typically the guy gets fired or quits and some manager shares the network-security access code, and then you're worse off. As for the rest of it, it's a job better suited to a security guard . . . or a nanny droid that's ready for the scrap heap."

Merei smiled at the thought of Auntie Nags standing over Imperial bureaucrats, her photoreceptors a continuous red.

"Anyway, I hope they're talking about that stuff in your courses and at whatever this early-morning club of yours is," Jessa said. "It's less glamorous than network traces and intruder traps, but it's more important."

"I've been studying it a lot recently," Merei said. "So I did okay, Mom?"

"Better than the security chiefs at some of Lothal's ministries," her mother said with a scowl. "They have a lot to learn."

I sure hope that includes the Transportation Ministry, Merei thought as she began to fold the napkins.

★ ★ ★

Zare had just sat down across from Jai when Currahee marched into the mess hall.

"CADETS! REPORT TO THE ASSESSMENT HALL IN FIVE MINUTES! HELMETS AND HARNESSES!"

"Didn't look that appetizing anyway," Jai said with a shrug as the boys left their nerf cubes and vegetable mash to cool and congeal without them.

"We should grab ration bars on the way out," Zare said. "Who knows what they have in mind or how long it will be till we eat."

"Quick night's march to Naboo?" Jai asked with a grin.

"Why stop there? Double-time it and we'll make Coruscant by dawn."

"I'll get two ration bars, then."

When they arrived at the assessment hall, a glowing flag stood atop the Pillar.

"This isn't even a challenge," muttered Oleg. "Instead of going down, we go up."

"But how?" Jai asked. "I don't see any handholds."

Zare dialed up the magnification on his video sensors, but there was nothing but the usual grid on the Pillar's sheer sides.

"CADETS! BEGIN!" shouted Currahee as the chime sounded in their helmets.

A low hum filled the room and platforms emerged from the sides of the Pillar, then began to rotate around its sides. The lowermost row was about a meter and a half above the floor and rotated left, the one above it rotated right, and then they alternated all the way to the top of the Pillar.

"See you at the top, losers!" crowed Oleg, springing atop a platform as it passed by.

A few seconds later Oleg said a word that would have earned him a demerit if Currahee or Chiron had heard it. Zare saw him sprawled on the floor below after his platform retracted.

"Have to be quicker than that!" Jai said, leaping onto a platform alongside Lomus, a beefy cadet from Unit Cresh. While Lomus tried to get his footing, Jai jumped and caught the edge of a platform heading the other way above him. The platform below him immediately retracted and Lomus crashed to the floor in a heap beside Zare.

Zare jumped onto the lowermost platform, waving his arms to keep his balance, then pulled himself up to the row above him and then the one after that. He saw Jai on the next platform, preparing to continue his ascent. But then the platform above Jai retracted, dropping a cadet onto his perch and knocking Jai to his knees.

Zare jumped up a row and looked down, expecting to see that the platform had retracted and dumped Jai and the other cadet. But they were both still standing there looking up at him.

"Something's changed," Zare said, activating his unit's channel. "The platforms aren't retracting."

A second later he felt the platform beneath his own feet begin to retract. He jumped blindly, catching the platform above him by his fingertips.

"Wrong as usual, Leonis!" Oleg chuckled.

"I stand corrected," Zare said as he hauled himself up.

"I know what's going on," Jai said, and a moment later he clambered aboard Zare's platform, holding up one hand. "Wait."

The two cadets readied themselves to leap away, but their platform remained motionless. Jai gave Zare a thumbs-up.

Zare shut off his helmet microphone and raised his faceplate. Jai did the same, looking puzzled.

"Why help Oleg?" Zare explained. "We'll go up together."

Jai grinned and the two of them ascended a row at a time, rising rapidly. Zare looked over and saw they'd caught up with Oleg, who was frantically jumping from one platform to the next as they retracted beneath him.

"You rigged the test somehow!" Oleg complained over their shared channel.

Zare laughed as he and Jai studied the remaining rows between them and the flag.

No, he thought. *We're just working as a team. Something you'll never understand.*

"He's figured it out," Jai warned as they reached the second row from the top. Zare looked over and saw Oleg had recruited Uzall, a cadet from Unit Besh. They were just one level behind them.

"Come on, we're almost there," Zare said. "Move on three. One, two, THREE!"

"Something's bothering me, though," Jai said. "Each assessment has three winners, right?"

"Right," Zare said. "Maybe for this one it's the top three teams. We'll find out in a moment, I guess."

The two of them jumped up to the top platform, then eyed the flag above them. One more leap should—

"Look out!" Jai yelled.

A split second later the platform retracted smoothly into the Pillar. Zare tumbled onto a platform a level below and wound up on his hands and knees, while Jai landed on his feet next to him.

"Come on, Zare, get up! The others are catching us!"

Zare tried to get his bearings. He heard Oleg laughing over the unit channel and looked up to see him shove Uzall down, then jump to the top platform. It remained stationary beneath him and he gave Zare and Jai a mocking salute before climbing the rest of the way to the flag.

The exercise was still bothering Zare when he finally got to comm Merei from one of the Academy's privacy booths.

"I mean, what kind of lesson does that teach?" he wondered. "First they emphasize teamwork, but then they punish it and reward selfishness. It doesn't make any sense."

"I don't get it either," Merei said from her bedroom. "Maybe it's a test."

"Everything's a test," Zare said. "Psych tests, and equipment tests, and assessment after assessment."

"That's not what I meant," Merei said. "I meant maybe they want to see which cadets are sufficiently aware to even ask the question you're asking, and raise it with their superiors. Which means you'll make a fine Imperial officer one day, Zare."

Zare glared at her, then realized she'd been joking. He sighed and crossed his arms across his chest.

"Sorry," he said. "I'm just tired and need to hit my bunk. What were you going to tell me? Something about tomorrow?"

Merei shook her head. "Don't worry about it. You've got a lot on your mind. Get some sleep, Zare. You need it."

Zare signed off, thinking miserably that it felt like Merei was on the other side of the galaxy instead of only a few kilometers away in Capital City. But the test kept bothering him, and he found himself heading toward Chiron's office instead of the barracks.

But another officer was with Chiron, standing beside his desk. The man turned and Zare's eyes widened. It was Roddance—the officer Zare had seen leading the deadly roundup of peaceful protestors in the Westhills a year ago.

"Well, if it isn't Cadet Leonis," Roddance said, his pale blue eyes bright and predatory.

"Lieutenant Roddance," Zare stammered. "This is a surprise."

"It's Captain Roddance now, Leonis," the officer said, tapping his rank badge. "How are the assessments going?"

"Fine, sir," Zare said. "Thank you for asking. I'm sorry, Lieutenant Chiron. I'll come back later, sir."

"No need for that, Leonis," Roddance said in his

smooth, cultured voice. "Chiron and I were cadets together, you know—there's nothing you can't say in front of both of us."

Zare glanced at Chiron, who gave him a thin smile.

"But let me guess," Roddance continued. "You were coming to ask about your sister, weren't you?"

Zare's eyes widened in surprise. Then he felt a surge of wild hope. Perhaps Roddance was there because the Empire had gotten whatever it wanted from Dhara and was now letting her go.

"I was just talking with Chiron about the subject, in fact," Roddance said. "He's been diligent in making inquiries at headquarters."

Zare nodded, but Roddance leaned forward, his eyes hard.

"I'll tell you the same thing I told him, cadet," he said. "The Empire is working to discover what happened, and you will be informed the moment there is something to report. Until that time, I suggest you both make better uses of your time than pointless worrying. Lieutenant Chiron has cadets to supervise, and you have assessments to focus on."

"Yes, sir," Zare forced himself to say.

"Very well, then," Roddance said, throwing a last glance Chiron's way before turning back to Zare. "My best to your family."

Then the officer was gone, trailed by the sound of his bootheels.

"My apologies, Zare," Chiron said, waving tiredly at a chair. "That wasn't the way I planned to update you about your sister."

"That's okay, sir," Zare said, trying to tamp down his fury at Roddance and the Empire he served.

"But it's a good sign that Captain Roddance learned of my inquiries and came to me to address the subject," Chiron said. "That shows the Empire is indeed taking a keen interest in Dhara's case."

Zare smiled thinly. Chiron might have meant well, but he was wrong—the Empire was indeed interested in Dhara, but its goal was for no one to find her. And Roddance had been sent to warn Chiron off.

"Anyway, I know that isn't why you came to see me," Chiron said, sitting up straight and seeming to recover his normal poise. "What's on your mind, Zare?"

For a moment Zare couldn't remember—the unexpected encounter with Roddance had startled him. But then the evening's exercise came back to him. He no longer wanted to talk about it, but Chiron was looking at him expectantly.

"It's tonight's test," Zare said. "First it rewarded teamwork. But the way to win was to go it alone, abandoning your unit mates. What's the lesson there, sir?"

Chiron brightened, and Zare knew immediately that Merei had been right.

"That's an excellent question, Zare," he said. "The dilemma is one every officer will face at some point—how do you weigh competing priorities when trying to complete a mission?"

"But the goals changed halfway through," Zare said.

"You'll find that happens on missions. There will be more such lessons, Zare. For now, know this—that you asked the question is yet another sign of your promise as a potential officer."

Zare nodded, and forced himself to thank Chiron. But then he hesitated.

"Oleg won the assessment because he naturally thinks of himself and not the rest of his squad," he said. "Is that also the sign of a promising potential officer?"

Merei found an empty bathroom near an exit in her classroom building, then ducked inside and changed out of her school uniform. She eyed her iridescent green pants and Phelarion School T-shirt with distaste, then sighed and began applying her makeup in the style favored by Capital City's rich girls. That was easy enough—it was the same riot of whorls and stripes that had been a fad on her homeworld of Corulag two years ago.

Lothal really is the sticks, she thought, slipping on cheap metal bracelets.

She shut the bathroom door behind her and slipped out onto the V-SIS lawn, donning her helmet and goggles and activating the remote that warmed up her jumpspeeder. She had two consecutive free periods—enough time, she hoped, for her visit to the Transportation Ministry.

And if I wind up in Imperial custody, getting written up for missing class will be the least of my problems.

She let her fingers rest on the trio of network drives in her pants pocket, then gunned the jumpspeeder's engine and shot out of the V-SIS parking lot, making her way through Old City and then past the new buildings springing up all over the outskirts of town. The Transportation Ministry was one of them, a slab of stone and glass surrounded by a tamed square of grass. Merei parked among the drab landspeeders and forced herself to stroll nonchalantly up to the entrance.

You go to Phelarion, she reminded herself. *You think you own the planet.*

"Can I help you?" asked a bored-looking man at the reception desk. He had the Outer Rim accent typical of a lifelong Lothalite.

"I'm Kinera," Merei said, her voice dripping with Core Worlds languor. "Kinera Tiree. My mother's assistant arranged for me to sell raffle tickets here today. It's for our auction to help Clone Wars veterans."

The man's eyes jumped from her makeup to her Phelarion School T-shirt, then scanned his terminal.

"I'm sorry, I don't see an appointment. You said your mother called?"

"Yes. Fondana Tiree, the education minister."

She showed him her book of tickets.

"I'm afraid the minister's office didn't make us aware of your visit," the man stammered.

Merei sighed and reached into her pants pocket for her comlink.

"I suppose I'll have to call my mother and figure out where there was a communications breakdown," she said. "Her office is very efficient, though, so I can't imagine it was on their end."

"I'm sorry," the receptionist stammered, looking worried. "I can't give you a pass without authorization, and nobody's signed off—"

"They told mother's assistant I wouldn't need a pass—I'm just supposed to set up shop in the cafeteria."

Relief bloomed on the receptionist's face.

"Oh, is that all?" he asked. "It's right down the hall— I'll buzz you in."

Merei reminded herself to give him a lofty nod as

she strode through the doors—a high-ranking minister's daughter wouldn't stoop so low as to actually appear grateful.

She sat in the cafeteria for a few minutes, waiting as a handful of bureaucrats came in for caf and snacks. A couple gave her a mildly curious look, but then returned to their discussions. When they left, Merei left the cafeteria and headed down the hall, waiting outside the door to a bank of offices.

A tall man in typical civilian garb came down the hall and pulled out his identification card. He glanced curiously at her.

"I'm selling raffle tickets," she said.

"Sorry," the man said. "I'd like to help, but—"

"No—um, the women's restroom in the cafeteria's out of service," Merei said, putting her hands behind her back so he wouldn't see they were trembling. "They told me to use the one in here."

The man shrugged and opened the door with his badge. Merei followed him inside, past a break station, and down a hallway to a large room filled with desks and network terminals. From outside she heard the buzz of maintenance droids, fighting their daily battle with Lothal's fast-growing grasses. A few workers looked up for a moment, then back down at their desks.

"Bathroom's that way," the man said and Merei nodded and smiled.

Alone in the bathroom, she took one of the network drives from her pocket and left it beside the sink, where someone might have set something down and then forgotten it. The little black device was empty except for a single file she'd named TRANSPORTATION MINISTRY—PROPOSED EMPLOYEE BONUSES. The file contained an actual data-grid of numbers matched to employee codes, but that was camouflage for the Gray Syndicate's snooper program, which would surreptitiously load itself onto the user's computer and go about its business, hopefully undetected.

Merei checked her makeup in the mirror and unlocked the door, risking a last glance back at the drive and its payload. She walked back to the break station, where she stopped to pour herself a disposable cup of caf. It was bitter and she grimaced, pouring in sweetener. Before she left, she let her second drive fall to the industrial carpeting and nudged it against the counter.

She exhaled and made her way back to the cafeteria, where she forced herself to sit for a few more minutes. She imagined every person who walked through the door would point at her accusingly, and every announcement over the comm system would warn of unauthorized devices and a building lockdown. But each new arrival was a bored-looking bureaucrat looking to break up his or her morning, and each announcement was some bit of bland Transportation Ministry business.

She left the third drive under a nearby table and walked out of the cafeteria, reminding herself not to hurry. She was just a few meters from the reception area when a voice behind her called out urgently.

"Kinera, wait!"

Don't run—it won't do any good, Merei thought. Her knees were shaking as she turned.

Oleg was still crowing about his victory in the previous day's assessment as the cadets spread out across the now-familiar terrain of the obstacle course in the Easthills.

"You okay, Zare?" Jai asked from beneath his raised faceplate. "Because you look terrible."

"Thanks," Zare said, but he knew it was true. He had slept horribly. He had dreamed that Dhara had returned home, explaining that she was sorry to have worried them, but the Empire had needed her for a secret mission, one that required her to disappear. Zare had woken up and felt relief flood him, only to realize that he wasn't staring at the ceiling of his bedroom in his parents' apartment, but peering at the featureless ceiling of the Academy barracks.

Currahee's voice crackled inside his helmet.

"Form up by twos and follow the coordinates in your heads-up displays," she ordered.

To their relief, Zare and Jai were paired together, while Oleg was assigned to Lomus, which he complained about over the unit channel until Currahee broke in to give him a pair of demerits.

Zare was glad to be spared Oleg's company, but as he and Jai hiked along he felt his misery settle over him.

"You ever wonder what all this is for?" Zare asked after making sure his microphone was off.

"What all what is for?" Jai asked.

"This," Zare said, spreading his arms to encompass . . . he wasn't sure, exactly. The helmeted cadets, the obstacle course, Lothal, the galaxy?

Jai just grinned.

"We're learning to become officers in the Empire's service," he said. "Out for a stroll on the beautiful planet Lothal, remember? But think about how hard that first week was, Zare. Now, we strip down E-11s, run ten klicks, and practice tactical formations before breakfast."

"Which is a banquet, of course," Zare said. "But why do you want to be an Imperial officer, Jai?"

"To get off Lothal, of course," the other cadet said with a laugh.

"No, really."

"Well, to see the galaxy," Jai said. "But also because the Empire made civilization work again. It defeated the Separatists—"

"The Republic did that," Zare objected.

"A Republic that had been transformed to fight the war, and became the Empire. It defeated the Separatists, stopped corruption, and now it's making the galaxy safe a system at a time, taking away planets from slavers and pirates. And bringing opportunity to places like Lothal. I want to be a part of that. Doesn't that make sense, Zare?"

Zare nodded, but his mind was churning. It was the same answer he would have given a year ago, before he found out that the Empire that had accomplished all those things was also the Empire that made children vanish and murdered peaceful protestors.

And turned good kids like Jai Kell into officers trained to support an evil regime.

"What is it, Zare?" Jai asked.

"Nothing," Zare said. "Just tired. Let's get to our coordinates and see what Curry has in store for us this morning."

The two cadets followed their nav units to an

outcropping of rock. Atop it rested an old-fashioned projectile launcher on a trio of legs.

"This thing is ancient," Jai said. "Clone Wars vintage."

Currahee's voice sounded in their helmets.

"By now you've found your launchers," she said. "I'm sending the coordinates of your targets to your heads-up displays. The automated ballistics programs on the launchers have been disabled, so you'll have to calculate trajectories by hand. And a word of warning, cadets—your targets are just twenty meters from the other pair of cadets in your unit. Try not to blow each other up—it's a lot of paperwork."

"Nice knowing you," Jai said. "Lomus is too dumb to make stormtrooper—no way he'll do the math correctly."

Zare laughed nervously and the two of them got down to the business of making their calculations on their datapads. They got the same answer, then double-checked them.

"Leonis and Kell ready to fire," Zare reported.

"Go ahead then, cadets," Currahee said.

Zare activated the launcher and a missile streaked skyward on a puff of propellant. A moment later he saw a cloud of dirt and smoke appear; a second later he heard the whump of the impact.

"Direct hit," Currahee said. "Good work. Now brace for impact."

Zare lay on his face next to Jai, wondering if it were the last thing he'd do. He felt the ground heave and heard the roar of the shell striking nearby, his helmet's audio pickups automatically dulling the sound to protect his ears.

"Good job, Oleg and Lomus," Currahee said as Zare and Jai rose to peer at the crater blasted into the ridge below them.

"I bet there's a hidden shield generator around here somewhere that would have kicked in if they missed," Jai said. "It wouldn't do to have the Academy blow up its own cadets."

"I hope you're right," Zare said.

But Jai's words gnawed at him. No, the Academy probably wouldn't blow up its own cadets. But it was willing to make them vanish and lie to their parents about what had happened. And the cadets who went on to the next link in the Academy chain would be trained to become enforcers of the Emperor's will, taught to lie and even to kill all those who opposed his rule.

Zare risked a glance at Jai. It seemed crazy to imagine the floppy-haired, happy-go-lucky boy next to him as an agent of evil. But perhaps Roddance had been like this once. They'd talked about how the cadets were changing, growing stronger and more resilient and skilled. But they hadn't talked about how else they might be changing, or what they might be becoming.

Merei turned, the blood draining from her face, and saw a red-faced woman in a civilian tunic and pants hurrying down the hall in her direction.

"Kinera! Miss Tiree!" the woman said. "I didn't get to buy a raffle ticket!"

Merei's shoulders sagged with relief.

"Oh, sorry," she said. "My datapad's card reader broke, so . . ."

"That's okay, I have actual credits," the woman said. "I'm glad I caught you before you left. I think it's so great what you're doing—it's such a good cause. Now, how much is a ticket?"

Merei fumbled for her ticket book, thinking she should have thought about the raffle beyond using it as an excuse for getting through ministry security.

Take it easy, she reminded herself. *Phelarion School, remember?*

"They're three credits each," Merei said. "I can write you a receipt and post it to the school network when I get back."

"And what are the prizes?"

"Top prize is a vacation on, um, Boranda," Merei said. "Then there's a full day at Old City Spa, a new datapad, and some other good things."

"Boranda!" the woman said. "I'll take five tickets, please. Oh, and I told my whole work group about the raffle. Here they come."

Merei found herself handing out tickets to a crowd of excited ministry officials. When the crowd finally dispersed, she waved to the receptionist, nearly a hundred credits jingling in her pockets.

The cadets were used to inspections, but on the morning of Visiting Day Currahee outdid even herself, checking every centimeter of their ceremonial uniforms—blinding white tops, gray trousers, and regulation boots that had been repeatedly polished.

Lomus had his tunic buttoned incorrectly and half of Unit Dorn was sent back to buff their boots again, but Currahee then declared them fit for viewing and hustled them to the waiting areas to either side of the stage in the amphitheater, now loud with the voices of parents and friends waiting to greet their cadets.

"I wish my Dad could see me today," Jai said, looking misty-eyed.

"Bah," said Oleg. "Whole thing's a sentimental waste of time."

"Are your uncles here, Oleg?" Zare asked curiously.

"Yes," Oleg said, and his face fell. He looked away and Zare felt momentarily sorry for him.

Then Currahee was among them, lips pressed together but eyes steely with unspoken warning. The cadets formed up by units and marched on stage as the anthem of the Empire blared.

A year ago, Zare remembered, he'd been out in the audience, looking at the stage and craning his neck to be the first to locate his sister. As always, Dhara had spotted him before he could find her.

He saw his parents now, and felt his breath catch at the sight of Merei's slim, pale figure standing between them. He smiled at them, adding a wink when Merei spotted him.

His father smiled broadly in return, but Zare saw the dark hollows under his eyes—Leo Leonis might still believe in the Empire, but his daughter's disappearance had weighed heavily on him. His mother's smile was tentative and her face was gray with worry. Zare knew what she was thinking: she'd lost a daughter under mysterious and sinister circumstances, and had then agreed to send her only remaining child to risk the same fate as his sister.

And where are you now, Dhara? I came here to find you, but what if it's too late? What if they've killed you, or taken you somewhere I'll never discover? How long will I have to pretend to be a good Imperial?

Commandant Aresko strode out to address the crowd, flanked by Currahee, Chiron, and Grint. Chiron caught sight of Zare's face and gave him a reassuring smile.

Automatically, Zare smiled back. The Imperial officers pivoted smoothly and the cadets snapped to attention as one, their reaction honed by weeks of drills and instruction until it was second nature.

The crowd murmured appreciatively, then began to cheer. And a disquieting thought crept into Zare's head and refused to be dislodged.

What if I play the role of good Imperial long enough that I forget it's a role?

After the assembly the cadets filed off the stage to greet their parents, then led them to the assessment hall for refreshments. Leo caught Zare up on the neighborhood gossip, while Merei was content to hold his hand and squeeze it periodically. Elsewhere, Zare saw Jai good-naturedly trying to wriggle out of his mother's latest tearful embrace, while Oleg sat in silence with two older men.

Tepha cleared her throat at Leo, who looked puzzled, then nodded. The two headed off to endure a sergeant's talk about the capabilities of AT-DPs. When they were gone, Merei grabbed Zare, kissing him and drawing a corrective bark from Currahee.

"I'm so glad to see you," Merei said. "It's been so long."

"I know. I feel the same way. I can't believe you're really here."

"I'm sorry I haven't made any progress," Merei said, then lowered her voice. "But I've just done something I hope will get us the answers we've been looking for."

Zare looked around, but Currahee had moved on and the blare of conversation was too loud for anyone to overhear them. Merei quickly told Zare what she'd done, then grinned.

"The snoopers worked," she said. "I've got the access codes of an Imperial personnel manager and a systems coordinator. The coordinator's access code let me give the personnel manager the ability to create new IDs with full security clearance."

Zare stared at her in shock.

"You'll get caught," he whispered.

"Unlikely," Merei said. "I switched the snoopers off once I had what I needed—they're dormant, almost impossible to find, and will erase themselves at the end of the week. Meanwhile, tomorrow morning an Imperial Security Bureau inspector will be added to the system, with access to nearly the entire network on Lothal. Technically, Zare, I think I'm about to outrank you."

Merei saluted.

"A year ago you never would have taken a risk like that," he said.

"That's no way to speak to a superior officer, Cadet Leonis."

"But what you're doing . . . it's incredibly dangerous," Zare said in a low, urgent voice.

"You think I don't know it's dangerous, Zare? But so is what you're doing. And wherever Dhara is, I guarantee she's in danger, too."

PART 3:
INFILTRATION

Zare disliked Unit Aurek's new cadet the moment he saw him.

Dev Morgan had untamed black hair, a cocksure grin, and a loose-limbed slouch that hid an easy grace. He was a transfer from the Pretor Flats Academy on the far side of Lothal, one of seven cadets brought in to replace those who'd washed out during the rigors of orientation.

"I'm Jai Kell—my family and I went to Pretor Flats one winter," Jai said from where he sat on the top bunk across from Dev. "Beautiful place. Did you grow up there?"

"Uh, here and there," Dev said. "There's not a lot to tell. I'm Dev Morgan and I'm here now to show you heroes what a real Imperial cadet looks like."

Zare looked over, annoyed by this display of braggadocio, but Dev threw them all a rakish salute and grinned. Jai grinned back and Zare shook his head. But Oleg glowered up at his new bunkmate.

"Watch your mouth or you'll be back at Whatever Flats before you can say 'Sir, yes, sir,'" he warned. "You're in the big city now, Morgan. You'll find we're stiffer competition than a bunch of moisture farmers with sunstroke."

"Sir, yes, sir," Dev deadpanned, then grinned again.

Jai laughed, but Zare turned his back, occupying himself with inspecting his E-11. Something was wrong about the new cadet—but Zare couldn't figure out what.

What if he's a spy? he wondered, eyeing Dev covertly. *Or, worse, what if he's part of a plot, like the one that ensnared Dhara?*

Despite all her preparations, Merei still hesitated before logging on to the Imperial network with her new credentials as an inspector for the feared Imperial Security Bureau.

She entered her access code and sat silently for a moment, imagining blaster fire shattering the windows of her bedroom as stormtroopers blasted the front door apart and clattered up the stairs.

But nothing happened. The screen cleared and she

was looking at the spoked Imperial symbol and a selection of ministries she could access.

Guess I better look around before the stormtroopers get here, she thought with a grim smile. *Let's see how much better the ISB's access is than what I had before.*

Merei navigated through screens until she reached the Academy's cadet records. She pulled up LEONIS, ZARE, then whistled appreciatively. Instead of basic information about Zare and his status as a cadet, she could see everything from medical exam results and personality test scores to assessment ratings and instructors' notes.

Are your ears burning, Zare? she wondered with a smile as she finished reading a glowing report from a Lieutenant Chiron.

"'Pending outcome of second-round assessments, Cadet Leonis is an ideal candidate for officer training,'" she read. "If they only knew."

She navigated back to the main portal for Academy records and typed LEONIS, DHARA. But her finger hesitated over the key that would send the command to the network. She wasn't exactly sure what she could access as an ISB inspector, and any information about Dhara would likely be much more sensitive than what was available for Zare. Triggering an alert could be devastating—while she'd camouflaged her queries' point of origin, a trace might turn up the curious fact that an ISB inspector was accessing the Empire's network through an anonymous connection.

She backtracked to the security ministry, scanning the day's law-enforcement alerts out of habit. She noticed that the day's arrest records included suspects' personal information, which her earlier inquiries had never turned up.

Merei sighed with relief. Her security clearance had to be pretty good.

More confident now, she typed a new name into the database: OLLET, BECK.

The arrest record she'd read many times came up first. But this time, there was another file, one she'd never seen before.

It read INTERROGATION RECORD/TRIBUNAL PROCEEDINGS.

She accessed it before it occurred to her to wonder if that was a good idea, then leaned forward to read, one hand over her mouth.

Beck had been hostile under questioning, but stuck to his story—he'd been a new recruit to a three-person resistance cell dedicated to bringing down the Empire because of its destruction of orchards in the Westhills and its violence against protestors. He didn't know the identity of the jumpspeeder rider who'd attacked the troops pursuing his group's landspeeder—probably an angry farmer, he'd said. And there was nothing about Zare or Merei.

The last line of the interrogation report read FOUND GUILTY BY SECURITY TRIBUNAL; ENROLLED IN PROJECT UNITY FOR EXPERIMENTAL RE-EDUCATION.

Project Unity? What's that?

Merei called up the Academy records and entered Dhara's name. Files scrolled onto the screen. She was familiar with the first few—basic Academy records, followed by school reports and immigration information. Below that were Academy files similar to Zare's.

And then, at the bottom, she read ACADEMY SPECIAL ASSESSMENT—CONFIDENTIAL.

Merei clicked on it.

A red box appeared on the screen. She stared at it, puzzled.

ACCESS GRANTED PENDING INPUT OF SINGLE-USE CODE FROM ZX-5 ACCESS DISK.

"Merei!" her father called. "Dinner's on the table!"

Merei rolled her eyes, annoyed.

"Okay, just a minute!" she yelled, logging out of her ISB account and shutting down the programs that concealed her inquiries to the Imperial network. Of all the times to be interrupted.

But then she brightened. She didn't know what an

access disk was, but she bet the two security experts waiting for her at the kitchen table did.

To her consternation, Merei's parents were in the middle of a discussion of Lothal politics when she sat down at dinner—a discussion that dragged on until Merei wanted to bring her fists down on the table and scream.

I'm the only kid in the galaxy who actually wants *her parents to ask how school went, and they won't do it.*

Finally Gandr looked over at her with one eyebrow raised.

"And why are you so fidgety?"

Merei reminded herself not to look eager—her parents should feel like they'd dragged the information out of her.

"Oh, just something at school that I'm trying to figure out," she said.

"Gotcha," Gandr said, then reached over and patted her hand. "I'm sure you'll get it, Mer Bear. Now, Jess, ask yourself what Governor Pryce would do if—"

"It's about when to use a ZX-series access disk," Merei said. "You know, the pros and cons of that approach."

Gandr and Jessa exchanged a puzzled look.

"I'm surprised one of your instructors would focus on that specific solution," he said. "Which ZX model were you discussing?"

"The ZX-5," Merei said.

"That's Imperial military stuff," Gandr said. "Totally overkill for civilian applications."

Jessa snorted. "I'll say. You'd have military intelligence all over you before you installed it. For civilian use you don't need anything beyond a basic decoder with decent encryption."

"Oh, so the ZX-5 is a decoder," Merei said.

"A very high-powered one," Jessa said, then launched into a discussion of encryption standards that Merei found baffling.

Gandr saw his daughter's puzzlement and smiled at her.

"Back to basics, Mer Bear," he said. "It's the basic security principle of something in the head and something in the hand. To access a sensitive file, you need your regular access code and the code displayed on the decoder, which changes every few seconds."

"So unless you have the decoder, you can't read the file."

"Right," Gandr said. "The more important the official, the stricter the orders about keeping his or her decoder on hand at all times, or restricting its use to a specific location."

Merei felt cold. Discovering what had happened to Dhara had just gotten much, much harder. Her ISB credentials allowed her access to that information, but only in conjunction with an Imperial decoder.

"There's a reason for all that security," Jessa said. "Criminals and dissidents are always trying to get access to the ministries. In fact, I was late because I've been ordered to investigate an apparent breach at the Transportation Ministry."

"What?" Merei asked.

"The Transportation Ministry," Jessa repeated. "Our security folks are still investigating how they got into the building and what network defenses have been penetrated."

"Any leads?" Merei forced herself to ask.

Jessa shook her head. "The first thing I did was request the cam-feeds, of course. But the idiots were only keeping two days of video archives, so what I wanted to see is gone. We spent the afternoon searching the network for unauthorized transmissions or rogue programs, but with all the inter-ministry activity that's a needle in a haystack until the weekend sweep runs. Tomorrow we'll start questioning the custodial crew—there's talk some of them had associations with gangs in Old City's alien quarter."

Merei tried to hide her shock. Her intrusion had been discovered—and her mother was leading the investigation. She forced herself to remain calm as she cleared the dishes and cleaned up the counters, then returned to her room and deleted the accounts she'd used to receive transmissions from her snooper programs.

Calm down, she reminded herself. *The snoopers are dormant, and they'll erase themselves from the network at the end of this week, before the anti-intrusion sweeps. They haven't found them yet, and even if they do, the transmissions no longer lead anywhere. Plus, there's nothing tying me to the phony ISB identity. I can delete that, or just stop using it.*

She'd be fine—well, as long as she got access to a high-powered decoder, completed her mission by the weekend, and wasn't somehow caught by the very capable Imperial security specialist who happened to be her mother.

When Currahee woke the cadets at dawn, Zare, Oleg, and Jai found themselves standing at attention before they even realized they were awake. But Dev was a moment late descending from his bunk, earning himself a face full of screaming Imperial sergeant.

"Today you go to Commandant Aresko," she growled, turning from Dev and Oleg to glare at Jai and Zare. "He's conditionally approved you to begin field training after winter break. He thinks you're ready to try your hands at being soldiers."

At the moment, Currahee looked like she didn't share that opinion.

"That means he'll be supervising the rest of the week's assessments personally—and only the most promising cadets will be tested," she said, leaning close to Dev. "If any of you make me look bad, I'll have you scrubbing floors and hauling trash before dawn every day for the rest of your term!"

"I guess she's not a morning person," Dev said as Currahee strode off to glower at Unit Besh.

"Neither are you, apparently," Oleg sneered. "Did they let you sleep in at the Yokel Flats Academy or whatever it was?"

"Sometimes," Dev said with a yawn. "It was a reward for winning assessments. Kind of like the three I won yesterday. And the two I won the day before that."

And there was that cocky grin again.

"Someday, Morgan," warned Oleg, pale with anger.

Jai laughed, and Oleg turned on him, jabbing a finger in his face.

"You too, Jai."

"That's enough, Oleg," warned Zare. But he was a bit annoyed himself. Dev had won five assessments over two days, and Zare couldn't figure out how he'd done it. He was quick and agile but not particularly strong, and Currahee had already reprimanded him twice for not paying attention. He just always seemed to be in the right place at the right time.

After a hasty breakfast Currahee handed Units Aurek and Besh over to Taskmaster Grint, who marched them into the assessment hall, barking at a couple of cadets from Besh who goggled at an AT-DP as it stomped past them. The massive blast doors were open, revealing Capital City beyond.

"And halt!" Grint ordered, facing Aresko where he waited on his command platform. "Squad NRC-077 for your inspection, sir."

"Cadets, you entered this facility as children," Aresko said. "And in a few short weeks, you will leave as soldiers. By the time you complete your training, you will be prepared to serve your Emperor. Today, we will test your strength and resolve. Are you ready to become stormtroopers?"

Behind the faceplate of his helmet, Zare scowled. Stormtroopers? Surely Aresko was testing them to see how they'd react. Aurek and Besh were the best units at the Academy, and all of their cadets were considered officer material.

A good cadet serves the Emperor as his officers think best, Zare reminded himself.

"Sir, yes, sir!" he shouted with the others.

"At ease," Aresko said, glancing at his datapad. Zare pulled off his helmet and exhaled, while Oleg glared at his rivals and Jai started joking around with Dev again.

"Who's under pressure?" Dev asked Jai, elbowing him in response to some taunt Zare had missed. "Not the guy who's won every assessment."

Zare tried to ignore the two cadets as they jostled each other playfully. A year ago Dhara had begun field training after winter break, spending an increasing amount of time away from the Academy. Then she'd vanished in the springtime, supposedly while during a training exercise.

Maybe that's when they'll come for me, Zare thought. *Maybe it's easier to snatch a cadet away from the Academy, where there are fewer eyes.*

Grint ordered Thurgos and Betancy out of formation, pointing at Currahee where she stood with Units

Cresh and Dorn. They removed their helmets and walked away, shoulders slumped. That left the four cadets from Aurek, and Giles and Uzall from Besh.

Suddenly the floor began to sink, leaving the six cadets staring up at Aresko and Grint.

"Cadets, you are descending into the Well and must climb out with all deliberate speed," Aresko said. "The winners will be given the honor of serving as aides in Imperial headquarters."

Zare's eyes widened.

"Those who lose will be serving Taskmaster Grint, and wish they'd stayed at the bottom of that Well."

"I'm taking that prize," Jai said.

"Not today, Kell," hissed Oleg, shoving Jai in the back. Dev put his hand on Oleg's chest.

"Back off, Oleg," he said.

"You, too, Morgan—you're both going down," Oleg said.

Dev glanced at the gridded walls of the Well and grinned. "Actually, we're going up."

Jai smirked at Oleg, who balled his hand into a fist and tried to push past Dev. Zare glanced up at Aresko, waiting for them to be reprimanded, but the commandant was just watching, a smirk lifting a corner of his mouth.

"The assessment begins in four . . . three . . . two . . . ONE!" said Grint, stabbing at his datapad.

Repulsorlift platforms emerged from the grid and began drifting across the Well above the cadets' heads, while others rose from the floor around them.

Dev sprang onto a passing platform, which dipped under his weight before resuming its course. Dev jumped onto another one, then leapt to grab a bar on the underside of a third moving in a different direction. Then he changed his mind and dropped down to a fourth platform.

"See you at the top!" he crowed as he leapt again.

"Yes, you will!" Jai retorted, scrambling after him. "From below!"

Zare rushed after them, looking for a pattern in the platforms' movement. It seemed completely random, yet there was Dev, turning unerringly to spot the next platform he needed to take him closer to his goal. And Jai was right behind him.

Oleg elbowed Zare hard in the side and Zare reminded himself to focus on making his own way out of the Well. Giles, meanwhile, was crouched on a platform rising quickly upward, turning from side to side to defend his prize.

"Failure is not acceptable," warned Aresko, his voice

amplified. "This Empire has no use for weakness."

Giles yelped. Zare looked over and saw blue tendrils of electricity climbing his legs. He plunged off his platform and landed several levels below, shaking his head woozily.

"Morgan, how do you do it?" Jai said over Aurek's shared channel. "It's like you know the platforms are coming before they're there."

"What can I say?" replied Dev even as he kicked off the wall of the Well, turning to land on a new platform as it emerged. "It's a gift!"

Dev and Jai were several levels above the rest of the cadets now, with Dev in the lead. As they passed each other going opposite directions, Dev reached down to help Jai onto his own platform. But neither of them saw Oleg behind them.

"You lose, Morgan," Oleg said, leaping at them. But before he could make contact, Dev and Jai jumped aside. Oleg plunged past Zare and the two Besh cadets, landing on his face far below.

Dev lifted his faceplate and offered the sprawled cadet a salute as Zare saw his chance and leapt desperately between platforms, trying to intercept one rising from the corner of the Well.

He was too late—Dev hopped out of the Well,

followed a moment later by Jai. Zare scrambled up behind them.

"Quite a finish, cadets," said Aresko. "It seems this trial was too easy. Morgan, Kell, you both set course records."

Aresko's eyes settled on Zare.

"And is it . . . Leonis?"

Zare forced himself to choke back his anger instead of rushing at the man who'd blandly assured his family that no effort was being spared to find Dhara.

"Sir, yes, sir," he managed.

"You three are today's winners," Aresko said. "But rest assured your next trial will be a greater challenge."

Zare was still steaming as he followed Aresko, Dev, and Jai through the corridors of the Academy to learn about their work assignment. A black astromech droid rolled past the quartet and Zare's eyes settled on it momentarily, curious to see such an old model in Imperial service.

Then he noticed the droid turn its head. He followed its gaze and saw Dev make a sign with his gloved fingers. The droid turned its head back and continued on its way.

Zare hurried to catch up with the others. It hadn't been his imagination—Dev had signaled to the droid.

★ ★ ★

"I know what Morgan's doing," Zare said when Merei answered the comm.

She looked at him in alarm.

"Where are you?" Merei asked. "Can we—"

"It's fine—we can talk," Zare said. "I'm in Imperial headquarters. This is Maketh Tua's office—I have access to it for deliveries. She's in meetings all day, and I know her comm panel isn't monitored."

It was Zare's morning rest break and Merei's free period, and she'd rushed home to talk with him. He could see the walls of her bedroom behind her, lit softly by the mid-morning sun.

"Okay, but slow down," Merei said. "Morgan. You mean the new cadet? Start at the beginning—you're going to blow a motivator."

Zare explained about Dev's peculiar gift of foresight, and how he'd seen him signal to the droid.

"He's getting information about the assessments from the droid," he said. "It explains everything."

"Except why a cadet would have connections like that," Merei said. "Let me think about it a minute. Besides, since we can talk I have something to tell you, too."

She explained quickly, watching Zare's eyes widen when he heard about Dhara's special assessment file. But she left out what she'd learned about Beck, and that her intrusion into the Transportation Ministry's computers had been detected. He had enough to worry about as it was.

"So I can access the file—but not without the decoder," Merei said.

"I might be able to help with that," Zare said. "As one of the winners of today's assessment, I have a work detail inside Imperial headquarters tonight."

"So you could get a decoder?" Merei asked, feeling a surge of wild hope.

"Maybe—wait, maybe not. Dhara said there were datapads that couldn't be taken out of certain rooms without raising an alarm. Would they have the same safeguards for your decoders?"

"Almost definitely," Merei said. "Let me see if I can find out about the security protocols there. Maybe I can find another answer."

"And what about Morgan?"

"Let me look," Merei said, typing and peering at her datapad. "Hmmm. All the official information you'd expect is there, starting with the Academy transfer, but it's the bare minimum. I mean, there's a record of a Dev Morgan attending school in Pretor Flats, and grades, but there are no tests or papers archived, and no teachers' notes."

"That seems really strange."

"It does, but it could be incorrectly keyed data or a botched file transfer. Let me look for him on the public networks. Hold on, Zare."

Zare waited impatiently, trying to divine what Merei was thinking from how she squinted and arched her eyebrows and bit her lip. That was distracting enough, but watching her face made him want to be with her, somewhere far from all this danger and deceit.

"There's basically nothing," Merei said. "A couple of user accounts with a fuzzy picture or two. No hobby sites, or comments about grav-ball or music, or any of the kind of history you'd expect a normal kid to accumulate."

"What does that mean?"

"It's like Dev Morgan doesn't really exist," Merei said. "I don't know about the droid, but whoever your new cadet is, he's not there to serve the Empire."

"Neither am I," said Zare. "But that doesn't mean he's on our side."

Zare, Jai, and Dev were only given a few errands before reporting to Imperial headquarters, but Currahee assured them that the various ministers and officers would find things for them to do—and that she expected them to make her proud.

When they emerged from the elevator, Zare waited until Jai had disappeared from view, then hurried after Dev, following the sound of the other cadet's boots.

He heard a murmur of conversation ahead of him and stopped. A moment later, the hard-eyed Agent Kallus passed by, carrying two datapads. Zare came to a halt and saluted, relieved when Kallus nodded absent-mindedly and kept walking.

Two datapads?

He hurried down the hall and turned right, hoping he remembered the way to Kallus's office. As he approached, he heard the hiss of a door closing ahead.

Dev had somehow gotten into the office.

Zare forced himself to wait outside the door. He wondered what the mysterious cadet would do when he was discovered. Would he deny everything? Come up with some story? Or try to subdue or kill Zare and flee?

The door opened and there was Dev with his usual infuriating grin. He had his helmet tucked under his arm.

"What do you think you're doing?" Zare asked, and smiled behind his faceplate when Dev started, his eyes widening.

Finally, something you didn't see coming.

They stared at each other for a long moment. Then

Zare heard a door open down the hall. He shoved Dev into Kallus's office and shut the door behind them.

The office was empty, and appeared undisturbed. Zare glanced around it, puzzled. What had Dev been looking for? Then he noticed the moonlight gleaming on something inside the cadet's helmet.

"Hey, get out of there," Dev objected as Zare extracted a silver square—an Imperial-issue decoder.

He's looking for the same thing I am, Zare thought. *But what does that mean?*

"I figured it would be something like this," Zare said, hoping to startle Dev into revealing himself.

"It's not what you think."

"I think this device has a built-in sensor, which would trigger *that*," Zare said, pointing above the door. "You try walking out with this thing, the whole facility goes on lockdown."

Dev looked up at the security sensor and his jaw dropped. Then he peered at Zare uncertainly.

"Wait . . . are you trying to *help* me?"

Zare held up the decoder, eyebrows raised.

"You really want to discuss this? Here and now?"

"Hmmm," said Dev, taking the decoder from Zare and sliding it back into its slot in Kallus's network terminal. "Not so much."

* * *

Once they were sure Jai and Oleg were asleep, Zare and Dev slipped out of the barracks and into a storeroom that Dev unlocked as deftly as he had Kallus's office.

"What do you need that decoder for?" Zare asked.

"My friends need it to stop an Imperial shipment," Dev said. "How'd you know about the sensors?"

"From my sister—Dhara," Zare said, staring down the racks of identical stormtrooper helmets. "She was the star cadet in this place. She knew the entire Imperial complex backward and forward."

"What happened to her?"

"They told us she ran off, but I don't believe it."

Part of Zare was amazed he'd revealed his secret—and to this mysterious infiltrator, of all people. But Zare felt oddly certain that Dev hated the Empire as much as Zare did. And he found himself relieved to finally speak the terrible truth about Dhara aloud.

But that still left the question of Dev and who he was.

"What were you doing breaking into Kallus's office?" he asked. "That's a great way to get shot."

"It's a long story, but I need that decoder."

So do I, thought Zare.

"And I could use a partner that knows his way around," Dev added.

"What's in it for me?" Zare asked.

Dev's eyes glittered.

"Do you really need a reason to mess with the Empire?" he asked, extending his hand.

Zare considered that. He still didn't know the whole story about Dev and this mysterious Imperial shipment. But he'd committed himself the moment he'd pushed him back into Kallus's office, instead of letting the alarm go off.

"No," he said. "I don't."

And he shook Dev's hand.

"Good," Dev said. "We have to finish in the top three tomorrow if we're going to get back inside Imperial HQ."

"Then let's do it."

He realized he'd been so preoccupied with his own anxieties that he'd barely said two words to Dev since his arrival. The other boy had probably forgotten his name.

"I'm Zare, by the way," he said. "Zare Leonis. And you're Dev, right?"

A flicker of emotion crossed Dev's face.

"Yeah. Yeah, that's me."

Liar, Zare thought. But it wasn't the time to investigate the mystery of Dev Morgan. Right then, he needed to strike some ground rules with his partner.

"I need to know what's so important about that shipment," Zare said. "And who these friends of yours are."

"Like I said, it's a long story."

"We've got all night," Zare said, crossing his arms over his chest.

Dev's face turned hard, but then he threw up his arms.

"The people I'm working with . . . they aren't friends of the Empire, let's leave it at that."

I know people like that myself, Zare thought, wincing at the memory of Beck Ollet's doomed rebellion and arrest in the marketplace.

"Go on," Zare said.

"The Empire's transporting part of a weapon in that shipment. Something big. The travel coordinates are encrypted—we need the decoder to discover them and intercept the ship that's carrying it."

"And when's this weapon of yours being transported?"

"Tomorrow," Dev said grimly. "If I don't get that decoder tomorrow, my mission fails."

Zare nodded.

"Thank you for leveling with me . . . Dev," he said, and suppressed a smile as the other cadet flinched at that name. "Now it's my turn. I need the decoder too."

"What for?"

"My sister, remember? My girlfriend's a slicer—a really good one, too. She's found files that contain the information about what the Empire did with Dhara. But she can't read them without that decoder."

Dev looked at the floor.

"If my friends don't stop that ship from getting where it's going, people will die."

"If I don't find my sister, she'll die," Zare said. "Everything I've done at the Academy has been about saving her."

The two cadets stared at each other. Zare spread out his feet, ready to receive a charge from Dev—or to tackle him.

"Wait," Dev said. "Maybe there's a way we can both succeed. My associates have a droid inside the complex."

Zare nodded. "An older-model astromech—I saw you signal to him."

Dev looked crestfallen.

"So that's where I messed up," he muttered. "I'm supposed to pass the decoder to him. He'll take it to my friends, outside the Academy. If your girlfriend can be in the same place, they can take turns."

Zare shook his head. Were they actually talking about taking turns, like stealing Imperial military secrets was a children's game?

"Who would go first?" he asked.

Dev dug in his pocket and held something up. It was Pandak's chance cube, Zare saw.

"I found it in the barracks," Dev said. "We can roll for who goes first."

Zare hesitated, then got down on his knees.

"I can't believe I'm doing this," he said. "I roll, you call."

He let the cube skitter across the floor.

"Blue," Dev said, wiggling his fingers for luck.

The cube came up blue.

"You always win," Zare said, but Dev just shrugged.

"Let's make sure we both win."

Morning found Units Aurek and Besh and three cadets from Cresh and Dorn at the bottom of the Well, with Aresko and Grint watching from their platform above. All the cadets had been told to report with their E-11 rifles.

"Today's assessment will be a little more challenging," Aresko warned. "You need to shoot the targets to activate the panels necessary to climb out."

Zare noted that sections of the grid sported bubble-like targets. He hefted his E-11 and waited as Grint counted down to the start of the exercise, then fired.

Direct hit! Blue sparks shot out of the target and a repulsorlift platform detached itself from the wall.

Zare ran across the Well as shots lit up the confined space, blaster bolts ricocheting crazily around him, and sprang atop a platform. Oleg was right behind him.

Zare fired and leapt onto a platform as Oleg landed on the other end. Before Zare could react, Oleg slammed into him and sent him flying, to land on a passing platform below. Zare winced and forced himself upright. Dev, he saw, was already halfway up the Well, firing with his usual uncanny accuracy.

Zare leapt and dragged himself up a level. Oleg was standing on a platform in the middle of the Well, firing not at the targets but at his fellow cadets' platforms. The impact made the platforms lurch, spilling cadets overboard.

Cheater, Zare thought. But it was an effective strategy—Dev and Jai were closest to the top of the Well, occupying a single platform. Then came Oleg, with Zare two levels below.

Zare saw Dev turn and look down—first at Oleg, and then at him.

"I'm not going to make it," Zare said bitterly.

Dev frowned in response, then winced—and shoved Jai in the back. The cadet landed on a platform below Zare, staring up the Well in disbelief as the rest of Aurek climbed out to stand in front of Aresko and Grint.

"Cadets, follow Morgan's example," Aresko said.

"There is no friendship in war. The only thing that matters is victory—victory at any cost. Tomorrow's final trial will push all of you to your limits. The reward for success will be a training session aboard an Imperial walker."

As Grint dismissed the cadets, Jai emerged from the Well and grabbed Dev by the arm.

"You sabotaged me!" he said.

"I did what I had to do," Dev said as he walked away. Jai didn't see the regret on his face. But Zare did.

A few hours later, Dev and Zare stood in Minister Tua's office inside Imperial headquarters, staring up at the ceiling.

"I hope your girlfriend's right about this," Dev said doubtfully.

"I've trusted her with my life every day I've spent at the Academy," Zare said. "If she says that vent leads to Kallus's office and that decoder, it does."

"Are you sure I can get it out through the vent without setting off the sensor?" Dev asked.

Merei had scoured the schematics and files for an answer to that question, without finding one.

"I'm . . . pretty sure," Zare said. "How are you going to reach anything from up there?"

"Don't worry," Dev said. "I've been training to become a Jedi."

"Yeah. Right. Who isn't?"

"You'll see," Dev said, as he leapt up to the ceiling hatch, then vanished inside.

Zare watched him go, then pulled out his datapad. His list of tasks was empty.

He took a deep breath and tried to calm himself. He'd crept over to Tua's office and commed Merei in the middle of the night to tell her about his hasty alliance with the mysterious Dev Morgan, and to ask her if she could slice a requisition order he could take to Kallus in the morning. He'd seen the fright in her eyes. Kallus was a real ISB agent, not a teenager impersonating one on a network. But she'd promised to try—and to meet up with Dev's mysterious allies outside the Academy that night.

That was almost as frightening—he imagined Merei being dragged off by stormtroopers, or shot in a misunderstanding upon encountering Dev's fellow operatives.

He shook the thought away. If they didn't get the decoder, there'd be no meeting. He had to focus on his own mission.

Zare exited Tua's office just as a pair of stormtroopers walked by on patrol. He stood at attention, then made his way to Agent Kallus's office. As he neared the door, his datapad beeped. There was a requisition order for Kallus.

Oh, Merei, I love you, he thought. Then he read the order she'd created.

You have got to be kidding me.

He pressed the indicator outside Kallus's door and heard the ISB agent tell him to enter. Kallus was sitting at his desk, working with a grim expression on his face. Zare tried not to let his eyes linger on the network terminal with the decoder inside, or the hatch above his head.

"Sir, your podracer parts have been delivered," Zare said. "If you just sign off here, I'll bring them up."

Kallus stared at him, then rose from behind his desk and strode across the room to stand in the doorway, staring down at Zare.

"Obviously there's been a mistake," he growled. "What would I want with podracer parts?"

"No mistake, sir," Zare said. "It says right here—two crates of secondhand podracer parts for Agent Kallus. That's you."

The hatch above Kallus's desk opened and Zare saw Dev's gloved hand appear. The slot on Kallus's network terminal popped open. Zare willed himself to keep looking at the ISB agent, which wasn't easy—Kallus was staring at him like a Loth-wolf that had cornered an injured whellay.

"I enjoy a good podrace myself, sir," Zare said as the decoder somehow rose from the desk and traced a path through the air toward Dev's outstretched hand.

Kallus stared at him, both angry and baffled. Zare tried to will him not to turn, to keep looking at the cadet who'd arrived at his door with a preposterous errand and not at the laws of physics being violated behind him. The decoder hung in the air for a moment, then shot into Dev's hand. The vent closed silently just as Kallus turned his back on Zare in disgust.

Zare's shoulders slumped in relief.

"So . . . are you going to sign it?" he asked.

"Cadet, are you ignorant?" Kallus demanded in a low, poisonous voice. "I said this is a mistake."

"Sir, yes, sir!" Zare said. "Sorry, sir!"

Zare expected Dev to take the decoder straight to his droid, but instead Dev said they had to talk—immediately. Which was fine with Zare—he had questions of his own. He followed the mysterious cadet to the storeroom, hands clenching into fists.

"How did you do that, back there?" he demanded

before Dev could even remove his helmet. "What are you?"

Dev pulled off his helmet and Zare saw he was pale with fright.

"Like I said . . ." Dev began, but Zare grabbed him by the front of his uniform, teeth bared.

"No more jokes, Morgan. What are you?"

"Zare, listen!" Dev said, trying to get free of the other boy's grip. "The Inquisitor is coming tomorrow night. For me and for Jai."

"The Inquisitor? Who's that?"

"An Imperial agent . . . one that makes Kallus look like a bantha calf."

"Don't tell me about Imperial agents," Zare growled, shoving Dev away. "For the last time—what are you?"

Dev smoothed his rumpled uniform, eyes lowered.

"I'll tell you. What do you know about the Force?"

"It was some kind of Jedi trickery," Zare said. "They used it to read minds and make people do things, back before they tried to take over the Republic."

"There's so much wrong with that I don't know where to start," Dev said. "But the Force is real. That's what let me levitate the decoder."

Suddenly it was all clear to Zare.

"This Force of yours is how you've won all the assessments!"

Dev nodded. "I can sense things through the Force—and so can Jai."

"And the chance cube roll?"

Dev looked embarrassed.

"Sorry about that. But don't you see? The assessments aren't just to train officers, but to find Force-sensitive cadets. Ones like me and Jai . . . and your sister, probably."

"But Dhara doesn't have powers like that," Zare said. And then his eyes grew wide. Hadn't Dhara always known where he was without looking? Hadn't she been able to sense what he was thinking?

Dev put a hand on his shoulder.

"That's why they took her," Zare said, thunderstruck. "And it's why they accepted me before any other cadet, and took me back even after I rejected them. My sister's Force-sensitive, and they think I am, too."

"Exactly," Dev said.

"But I'm not," Zare said. "I can't do any of the stuff you can do. Or that my sister could do."

"Right now that's not something to be sad about," Dev said. "I have to get the decoder to our droid. The original plan was that I'd escape with him, but now I'm staying. There's no way I'm letting the Inquisitor get his hands on Jai."

★ ★ ★

The stars were spilled across the sky as Merei crept through the narrow streets below the white towers of the Academy. She didn't see the hulking, purple-skinned alien until he stepped out of an alley less than a meter from her.

"Call me Spectre-4," he rumbled as a slim girl in riotously colored Mandalorian armor strode out of the shadows behind him.

"Uh, call me . . . Merei-1," Merei said.

"This is the cadet's slicer girlfriend?" the Mandalorian girl said doubtfully.

"That's right," Merei said. "And you are?"

"Nobody you want to know."

"Now, now," the massive Lasat chuckled. "You can call her Spectre-5. When our droid gets here, we get the decoder first. That's the deal."

"I know," Merei said. "I just hope you know what you're doing. We don't have a lot of time."

The Mandalorian girl jabbed a finger at Merei, but then held her hand to her ear.

"Spectre-3's on his way," she said, turning her gargoyle helmet to Merei. "Back off. This is our operation."

"I need that decoder, too," Merei said.

"Not till we're done with it," the girl said.

"Everybody relax," the alien said. "Just give us a

moment for a private conversation, girlie. We ain't gonna run off on you—a deal's a deal."

Merei didn't like it, but a glance at the alien's rifle told her she didn't have a choice. She walked into the alleyway and waited until the buzz of conversation had died away, then emerged to find the Mandalorian girl typing frantically at a datapad while the big alien stood watch and a battered astromech waited with ill-concealed impatience.

"Everything okay?" Merei asked.

"Well enough," the alien growled. "Complication with Ezra—um, with our agent. He's staying put for now."

"Oh," Merei said. She hoped that meant Zare was all right. "When will you be finished?"

The Mandalorian girl looked over her shoulder and Merei could feel her glower through the helmet.

"When I'm finished," she said. "I'm using the decoder as the seed for a decryption subroutine. If you know what that means."

"I sure do," Merei said. "I also know you can double that subroutine's execution speed by shutting down your datapad's diagnostics. They burn up a lot of processor capability."

"I'll do that," the girl said, her gaze resting on Merei a moment longer. "Thanks."

"Whatever you're doing, do it fast," growled the alien. "I love giving a few bucketheads an evening knuckle-polish, but tonight we ain't got time for recreation."

"You can relax," Merei said. "I tapped into the security drone network for this sector. I can see what they see—and if any stormtroopers head this way I can divert them."

"You can do that?" the alien asked.

Merei just nodded.

"Finished," the Mandalorian girl said a minute later, handing a silver square to Merei.

She slotted the decoder into her own datapad and navigated through the Academy files to Dhara's records, typing in the single-use code generated by the decoder and transferring the mysterious special-assessment file.

"Hurry," the armored girl said. "Spectre-3 will have to take it back before it's missed."

"I'll be finished when I'm finished," Merei said, transferring the other locked files from Dhara's records. "I have to make sure I can actually open them. Unless your friend wants to steal the decoder again."

"Not a chance, sister," the alien grumbled.

"Got them," Merei said. "I'll be done in a moment."

She opened the special-assessment file and paged through it.

This is what we went to all this trouble for, Merei

thought, trying to make sense of what she was seeing. *I can't believe I'm reading it in a Capital City alleyway with some prickly Mandalorian and a big slab of purple beef.*

"Did you get the information your friend needs?" the Mandalorian girl asked, sounding slightly friendlier now.

"I don't know," Merei said. "I need to make sense of this. But I hope so. Oh. You need the decoder."

She handed it to the Mandalorian girl, who bent and placed it in the astromech's grasper arm, then patted his head.

"What will you do now?" Merei asked.

"Wait until our friend can get away," the alien rumbled.

"Oh," Merei said. "Give me a comm code. I'll watch the drone network for you and contact you if you need to move."

The alien grinned, then reached down and tousled Merei's hair. The Mandalorian girl favored her with a nod, while the astromech extended a stubby arm and threw her a jaunty salute.

Jai didn't believe them.

"No—no way," he said, staring at Dev and Zare in their storeroom lair. "This is just another dirty trick. You're trying to get me busted out of the Academy."

"Uh, yeah," Dev said. "But not the way you think. The Inquisitor—"

"Please," Jai said. "I don't believe this Inquisitor exists. And even if he does, then maybe it's a good thing. The Inquisitor trains me, I get a top rank in the Empire . . ."

"Kell, you got a family?" Zare asked from where he'd been watching the argument.

"It's just me and my mother," Jai said.

"And how would she feel if she never saw you again?" Zare asked, crossing the storeroom to look in Jai's eyes. "My sister disappeared from this place, and I'm betting it was the Inquisitor who took her away. So unless you're ready to say bye to Mom forever . . ."

Jai reared back, startled—and frightened. He looked at Dev and Zare for a long moment, looking for a way out and finding only grim faces.

"Okay," he said. "What's the plan?"

"Simple," Dev said, putting his arm around the other two's shoulders. "The three of us have to win tomorrow's challenge."

"Not so simple," Zare said.

"How's that going to get us out of here?" Jai asked.

Dev smiled. "Because it gets us inside that walker."

★ ★ ★

Zare didn't have the Force as his ally, but all things considered, he thought he was getting pretty good at making his way out of the Well. He was a level below Dev, with Jai right behind him, and he had a clear path to the top.

Which was when Oleg raised his E-11.

Dev jumped down to shove Jai out of the way, and Oleg's blast caught him in the chest, knocking him off Jai's platform. He landed heavily, yelling for the others to keep going. Zare looked down, but saw it was no use. He climbed up to the floor of the assessment hall a moment after Oleg, with Jai third. Dev was fourth.

"Well, well," Aresko said. "Cadets Kell, Leonis, and Oleg win the day."

He turned to indicate the AT-DP standing over them on its stilt legs.

"And the prize," he said.

"You were supposed to be on the walker with us," Zare heard Jai say to Dev in a low, urgent voice. "Now what?"

"Stick to the plan," Dev said. "I'll figure out a way to get on board."

As they raised their faceplates, Zare gave Dev a worried look. But the rogue cadet just grinned his infuriating grin, and looked to the right. Zare followed his eyes and noticed the astromech zipping between the other AT-DPs parked in the assessment hall.

The interior of the AT-DP was cramped—three cadets and an Imperial pilot barely fit in the cockpit.

"So these control movement, and this fires the cannons," Zare said, gesturing over the pilot's shoulder. "But what are these?"

"Gyroscopics," the man said. "Here, I'll show you."

Oleg leaned forward, fascinated. As the pilot demonstrated the walker's function, Zare caught Jai's eye and slipped the Imperial's blaster smoothly out of its sling on the man's seat, then handed it surreptitiously to Jai.

Perfect grav-ball handoff, Zare thought. *Coach Ramset would be proud.*

Suddenly an explosion in the plaza outside the blast doors rattled the walker.

"What was that?" the pilot asked, rising out of his seat to peer through the viewports.

"My signal," Jai said. He raised the stolen blaster and stunned the pilot, who slumped to the cockpit's deck.

"What are you doing?" screeched Oleg. He leapt at Jai, who turned coolly, catching him with the blue concentric circles of another stun bolt as Zare climbed into the pilot's chair.

"Guess there's no turning back now," Jai said.

"No," Zare said.

Through the viewports he saw Aresko shouting orders into a comlink, while cadets ran back and forth, unsure what to do. The blast doors began to descend.

"Look!" Jai yelled. "Do something!"

Zare grabbed the joysticks, trying to remember what the now-unconscious pilot had shown them, and the walker began striding forward awkwardly. He found the cannon controls and sent a fusillade of bolts at the blast doors, catching another AT-DP that had responded to the earlier explosion. Zare's guns blew apart its drive engine and the machine crumpled, landing in the blast doors' path.

"Zare, watch out!" yelled Jai.

A troop transport in the plaza turned around and began firing at their AT-DP. Energy crackled over the bow cannons and the head of the walker slumped forward.

"Fire back!" Jai demanded.

"I'm trying!" Zare said.

He got the walker moving again, marching steadily toward the doors as laser blasts burst around them.

"Well, they've figured out which side we're on," Zare said.

"Terrific."

Someone was banging on the hatch.

"Oh, no," Zare said.

Jai readied his blaster rifle—but then they heard a familiar voice over their unit channel.

"Let me in!" said Dev.

The troop transport raked them with scarlet bolts of fire, aiming at the AT-DP's relatively weak ankle joints. The walker shuddered and the lights on Zare's control board turned an ominous red. He fought to stabilize the craft, then threw up his arms to protect his face as the walker toppled over face-first and slid across the floor of the assessment hall, the blast door settling atop its battered cockpit with a thump.

Zare struggled to free himself from the pilot's harness, then crawled over Oleg toward the hatch.

"You all right?" he asked Jai.

"Never been better," Jai said wearily.

Zare tried the hatch. It was stuck shut. He hit it with his shoulder, grunting in pain, and on the third try the hatch popped open. Dev was waiting on the other side. So was a girl in colorful Mandalorian armor. Stormtroopers were lying motionless in the plaza in front of the troop transport.

"You guys okay?" Dev asked as he and the Mandalorian girl helped Zare and Jai down. The little astromech droid rolled to a halt nearby, honking urgently.

"Yeah," Jai said. "Let's just get out of here."

But Zare stopped.

"Wait," he said to Jai. "Give me that blaster."

Jai handed the rifle over, looking curiously at Zare. "Uh, sure. Why?"

"Because I'm staying."

"What?" asked a shocked Dev.

"It's the only way I'll ever find my sister," Zare said.

"We've got bucketheads inbound!" the Mandalorian girl shouted, looking behind them into the assessment hall.

"I'll keep in touch," Dev promised. And then he, Jai, the Mandalorian girl, and the astromech were racing across the plaza. A civilian landspeeder braked to a halt and they leapt aboard.

Zare raised his blaster and began to fire, his shots hitting to the left and right of the speeder and ripping craters in the pavement. By the time Aresko, Grint, and a squad of stormtroopers reached his side, the speeder had accelerated and shrunk to a dot.

EPILOGUE:
THE INQUISITOR

Chiron waited with Zare during the hours he spent on lockdown.

He began by telling Zare how proud he was of him, and assuring him that he shouldn't blame himself for what had happened. No one had imagined that cadets Kell and Morgan might be traitors, willing to attack Imperial soldiers and destroy equipment. Zare had behaved heroically, against overwhelming odds, and almost managed to bring the enemies of the Empire to justice all by himself.

Zare accepted this praise with what he thought was the proper mix of pride and stoicism, then told Chiron that he was okay, and the officer shouldn't feel like he had to worry about him or babysit him.

Chiron just smiled sadly, and then Zare understood: he did need to babysit him. Those were his orders. They were waiting for something—or someone.

Then Zare realized: the person they were waiting for was the Inquisitor, the mysterious Imperial agent Dev had spoken of so fearfully. He was on his way to Lothal, except instead of Dev and Jai, he would be speaking with Zare.

After that he and Chiron said nothing. Zare alternated between wondering if Merei was all right and trying as hard as he could to think of anything else. Chiron just sat staring at the floor, passing his officer's cap back and forth in his hands.

Finally the door chimed and Commandant Aresko entered, lines of worry etched around his eyes and mouth.

"Come with me, Leonis," he said, not unkindly. "Don't be afraid."

It was those words more than anything that sent fear through Zare's heart.

The Inquisitor was waiting in Kallus's office, standing with his back to the door. He was a tall dark shape against the setting sun. Kallus stood nearby. When Aresko and Zare entered Kallus turned and studied the cadet for a long moment. Then he turned back to the window and the endless plains of Lothal.

"This is a black mark, Commandant," the Inquisitor said at last, lowering a datapad that he'd been studying and looking over his shoulder at Zare. "I don't know this boy, but this other one I know."

Zare stared at the slim, deadly-looking being. His skin was gray, like stone, but his eyes were a fiery yellow. They reminded Zare of burning coals, and his smallest movement suggested power kept in check.

And he was angry. Zare could see his rage in the way he held out the datapad to Aresko, its screen filled with an image of Dev. But he could also *feel* it—it seemed to flow out of the Inquisitor, like ripples from a rock hurled into a formerly quiet pool.

The Inquisitor thrust the datapad accusingly at a stricken-looking Aresko.

"This is the Padawan I encountered on Stygeon Prime," he said.

"That is Morgan," Aresko said. "The other was Kell. Cadet Zare Leonis here came very close to stopping their escape. He was part of the traitors' squad and knew them well—or thought so."

Zare tried to nod. The Inquisitor's terrible eyes remained fixed on him as a smile creased his gray skin.

"How admirable," the Inquisitor said. His voice was smooth and cultured. They might have been discussing some aspect of philosophy, or the latest opera from Coruscant.

He strode around the desk and Zare fought the urge to flee. The Inquisitor stared down at him, teeth bared.

"Well, Leonis," he said. "Let's take a walk, shall we? I want to know everything about your former friends."

Zare looked up into those burning eyes and could only nod.

The two of them walked through the headquarters complex to an interrogation room, every Imperial coming to a stop and standing at attention until the Inquisitor had passed.

Keep your cool, Zare told himself. *He's not interested in you, and you've done nothing wrong. You're the hero cadet.*

But his thoughts were screaming at him. This was the being who had ordered his sister to be taken away from the Academy and her family. Perhaps that face was the last one she had seen before she died.

The interrogation room was dim and quiet. Zare nervously eyed a bulbous black droid sitting on its perch in the corner, bristling with needles and probes. But the Inquisitor simply motioned for him to sit.

"Now tell me everything about Morgan," he said.

Zare could feel the being in his head somehow—he sensed the presence of another mind sorting and sifting through his emotions and seeking his thoughts. The faintest touch of that mind made him want to run and hide.

Zare began talking about Dev, about his doubts about the cadet and who he was. He could feel that other mind's hunger, its greed. He told the Inquisitor about Dev's skill at assessment after assessment, and how Zare had grown certain the new cadet was cheating.

All of those things were true, and he knew they were what the Inquisitor wanted. And maybe, just maybe, they would be enough to keep him from delving deeper, into the things Zare desperately needed to keep secret.

"But there was something not right about this Morgan," the Inquisitor said. "You're a bright young man—you must have sensed something."

Yes, Zare agreed hastily. He told the Inquisitor how Dev had never talked about himself or his family, and how sometimes he didn't respond to his own name.

The fiery eyes blazed even brighter and Zare looked away, fearful of becoming trapped in them.

"There is no Dev Morgan," the Inquisitor growled. "There never was."

What would the perfect cadet say now? Zare asked himself. *Come on, think!*

"Does that mean his victories in the assessments will be vacated, sir?"

"Ask the commandant," the Inquisitor replied, striding away from Zare with his hands behind his back. Zare felt that cruel intelligence withdraw and knew the Inquisitor now had no more interest in Zare than he did in a Loth-rat fleeing into a sewer pipe in Old City.

He doesn't care about me because he's seen the assessment results, Zare thought. *He doesn't think I can use the Force the way Dev and Jai did. And the way Dhara did.*

And then an awful realization struck him: his best chance to find Dhara—perhaps his *only* chance to find her—was for the Empire to think he shared her gifts.

"Sir?" he asked timidly. "There was something else. Something . . . strange. While we were aboard the walker, I felt like something was wrong somehow. Like Dev and Jai were hiding something. Like they were enemies."

Those blazing eyes turned on him again, and he felt the Inquisitor's hunger rising, like something boiling.

"If only I'd paid attention to that feeling, maybe I could have stopped them," Zare said.

"Your sister is Dhara Leonis," the Inquisitor said with chilling calculation. "Isn't that right, cadet?"

Zare forced himself to nod.

"It's a shame your sister ran away from the Academy," the Inquisitor said. "What an unfortunate end for what had been a promising career. You have my sympathies, cadet."

The being turned away, and Zare hesitated, knowing he stood on the edge of an abyss.

And then he leapt.

"My sister isn't dead," Zare said. "I know it. I can feel her out there somewhere, calling to me."

The Inquisitor turned, and Zare forced himself to remain still, to wait. If Dhara was dead, he had signed his own death warrant—and Merei's, too. The Inquisitor would smash his mind into fragments and extract everything he wanted to know, shredding every lie he had told, and exposing every secret.

The Inquisitor said nothing, but Zare could feel that vast and cruel intelligence focused on his.

"Dhara and I have always been able to sense each other, somehow," Zare said. "We never told anybody that. Because it doesn't make any sense, does it?"

The Inquisitor's eyes glittered in the darkness.

"It does make sense, cadet," he said. "In time, you will understand why."

When Zare finally appeared on the screen of Merei's datapad she gasped: his face was gray and there were dark hollows beneath his eyes. He was exhausted, but there was something else—something in his eyes she didn't recognize.

"Are you all right?" she asked. "I've been so worried."

"So have I," Zare said. He looked away for a moment, then wiped at his cheeks, blinking. Merei realized tears were running down her own face.

Then Zare began to laugh.

"I got a commendation," he said. "For saving the Academy."

Merei just stared at him. And then she began to laugh, too.

Zare finally stopped and pressed his palms against his eyes. He sat with his head bowed for a moment, and when he looked up again his face was grave. But there was something else there, too.

It was hope.

"Dhara's alive," he said.

"I know," Merei said. "You didn't give me a chance to tell you."

Zare's eyes widened.

"So tell me."

Merei's father was calling her from downstairs. Her mother had been working late, and they'd held dinner for her. She must have just come home.

"I'll be right down!" Merei yelled, then turned back to

Zare. "It's called Project Harvester. Dhara was removed from the Academy after meeting the program's special criteria."

"Meaning they found out she could use the Force," Zare said.

"The Force?" Merei asked.

"I'll explain later," Zare said. "Do you know where they took her?"

"Yes. Project Harvester is run from a secret installation on the planet Arkanis, one connected to Imperial headquarters there—and the Arkanis Academy."

"Then that's where I need to go," Zare said. "You're an agent of the Imperial Security Bureau—I don't suppose you could arrange a midyear transfer for me? Talk in the mess hall is that's been done on occasion, for exceptional cadets."

"No," Merei said. "The Empire would realize almost immediately that it wasn't legitimate, and start investigating how it happened."

Zare nodded. Gandr was calling more insistently now.

"In a minute, Dad!" Merei yelled.

"I'll have to get to Arkanis on my own then," Zare said. "By being the best cadet on Lothal. The goal has changed, but the mission's the same."

"I know," Merei said. "We'll make it happen. Be patient, Zare. Now, you need to sleep more than any person I've ever seen."

Zare nodded and broke the connection, smiling at her as he did so. Merei sat staring at the blank screen for a moment, then hurried downstairs.

"Sorry I'm late," she said, and then realized something: her snoopers had erased themselves from the Imperial network nearly an hour ago. Tomorrow's sweeps would find nothing. She sighed and let her shoulders relax, smiling at her parents. She had found the information Zare had needed, and how to read it, and now all traces of how she'd done it had disappeared.

"And how was your day, Mom?" Merei asked.

Jessa glanced over at Gandr and shrugged.

"We were just talking about that," she said. "That intrusion case at the Transportation Ministry turned out to be more interesting than I thought. We located the programs the attacker installed this afternoon— they were set to transmit data to an outside account."

Merei held her breath.

"We started figuring out how to isolate the programs, but either they were primed to detect that or were set to delete themselves on some kind of timer," Jessa said. "I have to admit, it was clever work."

Merei nodded, trying not to smile. It had been close, but she had escaped.

"But sometimes you need to be lucky as well as clever," her mother said. "Two of the programs deleted themselves before my team could isolate them, but the third was loaded onto a network terminal with a faulty chronometer. So its timer never went off, and we were able to freeze it and preserve the code. Once we trace where it was sending its transmissions, we'll be able to search accounts there—first the active ones, and then the ones that were deleted."

"I didn't know you could do that," Merei said in a small voice.

"Not many security experts could, Mer Bear—but luckily your mother's one of them," Gandr said.

"Yes, I am," Jessa said. "I don't know who these intruders are, but we're on their trail. We'll find them. And when we do, they'll find out what it means to face the wrath of the Empire."

ABOUT THE AUTHOR

Jason Fry is the author of *The Jupiter Pirates* young-adult space-fantasy series and has written or co-written some two dozen novels, short stories, and other works set in the galaxy far, far away, including *The Essential Atlas* and *The Clone Wars Episode Guide*. He lives in Brooklyn, New York, with his wife, son, and about a metric ton of *Star Wars* stuff.